Beauty & the Dragon Beast

Luna Rains

Beauty and the Dragon Beast

Shifter Royals: Fairy Tale Fated Mates

Luna Rains

Published by JL Lam Publishing, 2024.

BEAUTY AND THE DRAGON BEAST

First edition. June 14, 2024.

Copyright © 2024 Luna Rains.

ISBN: 979-8224660841

Written by Luna Rains.

Also by Luna Rains

Enchanted Ever Afters
The Arrow and the Axe

Fated Mates Saga
Fated Mate Surprise Daddy
Fated Mate Triplets Daddy
Fated Mate Secret Babies
Fated Mate Secret Twin
Fated Mate Twins Reunited
Fated Mate Witch's Prophecy
Fated Mate Prophecy Fulfilled

Shifter Royals: Fairy Tale Fated Mates
The Dragon's Magical Mate
Beauty and the Dragon Beast

Standalone
The Sword & the slipper

Watch for more at https://jllampublishing.com.

Table of Contents

Prologue: The Curse 1

The Shadow of the Curse 8

The Dragon's Heart 15

The Cursed Prince 25

The Call to Adventure 36

The Trial of Fire 46

Rival Encounters 57

Flashbacks and Secrets 67

Transformation and Revelation 77

Forged in Ice and Ice 87

Bloodied Ice 96

Reborn Through Love 103

The Heir's Legacy 114

Gathering Shadows 121

Kindled Courage 130

Forged in Frost and Flame 142

Dragonfire's Defiance 151

Prophecy's Dawn 159

Triumphant Unity 165

New Dawn, New Hope 176

Legacy Renewed 185

To my beloved husband,

Whose unwavering support, endless encouragement, and steadfast belief in me have been the guiding light throughout my journey.

Your love is the foundation upon which I build my dreams.

Prologue: The Curse

Freya, the Ice Queen

In the dim light of her prison, Freya's fingers traced the ancient runes she had etched discreetly into the stone floor. The cell was silent except for the soft whisper of her incantations—a sinister symphony of dark magics she had gathered over the years, each word and gesture bending to her iron will.

"They think they have seen the last of my power," she muttered, the shadows seeming to lean closer to listen. "They think they have stripped me of my reign and my vengeance. Fools."

Her mind, ever sharp and cunning, had pieced together a curse from the forgotten corners of dark magic—a spell potent enough to twist destiny itself. "Let them have their moment," she sneered, the plan crystal clear in her mind's eye. "It will sweeten the despair to come."

Her hands moved with precision, drawing energy from the vestiges of power that lingered in the forgotten spells bound into the walls of her cell. This curse, her masterpiece, would be her revenge. On his 18th birthday, the young prince they cherished would transform into a hideous dragon, forever torn between his human heart and the monstrous form he would be forced to bear.

"This will be my legacy," Freya declared, her voice a chilling promise to the cold stones around her. "Let him be a monster in their midst, let his pain be a mirror of my own betrayal."

She envisioned the prince, beloved and revered, becoming a creature of nightmare, his despair a permanent scar upon the kingdom that had dared to reject her. "They will wish for death before I am done with them," she whispered, her eyes glinting with malice.

As she completed the curse, the air in her cell grew colder, the very essence of her spite frosting the bars of her window. She laid back against her cot, a smile creeping across her face—a smile as cold and unforgiving as the fate she had woven for young Eirian.

"Sleep well, young prince," she hissed into the darkness. "Enjoy your fleeting days of sunlight and smiles. My shadow will fall upon you soon enough, and no light will save you from the darkness I bring."

In the chill of her cell, Freya stood poised, her senses tuned to the faintest murmurs of energy that seeped through the ancient stones. Weeks, months, years—time had honed her patience and her power, not dulled it. "Tonight," she breathed into the darkness, her voice barely a whisper, "the frost will spread beyond these walls."

Her fingers traced the intricate patterns she had secretly etched into the floor, patterns charged with dark energies gathered over countless silent hours. With a final, whispered incantation, she unleashed the pent-up power. The air crackled around her, a storm of suppressed magic waiting to erupt.

As the guards outside her cell shifted uneasily, Freya struck. She channeled the residual dark energy into a fierce pulse of force, a silent scream of power that shattered the magical restraints binding her. The cell door buckled under the sudden frost that spread like wildfire across its surface, the metal groaning and splitting as if crying out in agony.

Stepping over the threshold, Freya felt the familiar rush of freedom. Her presence alone was a wave of chilling energy, pushing back the guards who came rushing towards the disturbance. "Back!" she commanded, her voice carrying the harsh bite of winter. The guards stumbled, slipping on the sudden ice that formed beneath their feet, their breaths visible in the air as they gasped in the suddenly frigid atmosphere.

She moved swiftly, her cloak a shadow flowing behind her, each step deliberate and powered by the fury of her long confinement. As she passed, the security spells meant to contain her sputtered and died, snuffed out by the overwhelming darkness she wielded.

Outside, the night air was a balm to her senses, crisp and cold, welcoming her with the promise of vengeance. She left a trail of frost in her wake, the grass crunching underfoot, each blade encased in ice. The palace that had been her prison now lay behind her, its walls no match for the storm she had become.

Freya paused at the edge of the forest, her eyes reflecting the moonlight, her heart beating a rhythm of impending retribution. "The queen returns," she whispered to the night, her voice carrying a new threat. "And this time, no cage can hold me."

In the veil of night, cloaked by a swirling mist that seemed to follow her very command, Freya glided silently through the palace gardens. The jubilant noises of the celebration ahead served as a stark contrast to the icy calm that surrounded her, a barrier between her and the world she once dominated. "Fools," she murmured, her breath a puff of frost in the warm night air, "to think they can guard against what they do not expect."

With each step, the mist thickened, wrapping her form in a ghostly shroud that made her nearly invisible to the festive revelers. She moved with purpose, her eyes sharp beneath the hood of her cloak, surveying the scene with a predator's precision. The laughter and music, the clinking of glasses—all of it grated against her nerves, a reminder of what she had lost and what she vowed to reclaim.

As she weaved through clusters of guests, her presence sent an involuntary shiver down the spines of those she passed. Unseen, unknown, her shadow brushed against a laughing couple, pulling a sudden gasp from them as an inexplicable chill swept over their skin. "Too close," they muttered, huddling closer, unaware of the danger that moved among them.

Freya's lips twisted in a grim smile as she neared the heart of the festivities. Here, the magic of the celebration was thickest, a tapestry of joy and unity that she ached to tear apart. She paused, letting the laughter wash over her, each note a spark against the cold fury within her.

"They celebrate their peace," she whispered to herself, her voice blending with the rustle of leaves in the breeze, "a peace built on my downfall. But tonight, the air changes. Tonight, the cold returns." With that, she stepped closer to the throng, her form hidden, her intentions as dark as the shadows that danced at her feet.

As Eirian's laughter pealed through the air, a bright focal point of youthful joy amid the festivities, it was abruptly cleaved by the chilling presence that materialized at the heart of the celebration. The mist that had been gently drifting among the guests suddenly coalesced, and with a crisp whisper of frost, Freya appeared.

The laughter died in throats, and the music faltered as if the notes themselves were frozen by her presence. Guests recoiled, their expressions morphing from jubilation to stark, palpable shock as they stumbled backward, their steps unsure and frantic. There, standing with the regal bearing that had once commanded their awe and fear, was their former queen, her silhouette sharply drawn against the backdrop of festive lights.

Her eyes, bright with a cold, calculating malice, swept over the crowd, resting finally on Eirian. A thin smile played upon her lips as she absorbed the ripple of terror her appearance wrought. "Did you think me vanquished? Forgotten?" Her voice, though no louder than a whisper, carried clearly, cutting through the silence like a knife.

"Look upon your celebration, your unity," she continued, her gaze piercing through the crowd to where Seraphis and Wynter, Eirian's parents, stood, frozen. "It is but a castle built on sand, awaiting the tide." Her laughter, cold and mirthless, echoed off the palace walls, as she stood resolute, a specter of vengeance poised to reclaim her narrative.

In the surreal stillness that followed her dramatic reveal, Freya's smile widened, a dark harbinger as her gaze fixed upon Eirian. With the crowd's attention riveted on her, a hush fell over the courtyard, the kind of tense silence that precedes a storm. She raised her hands, the air around her crackling with the latent dark energy she had harnessed from years of confinement and planning.

Freya surveyed the crowd with a disdain sharpened through years of confinement. The vibrancy of the celebration, a stark contrast to the darkness she embodied, only fueled her contempt.

"Behold, the future wrought by your so-called peace," she intoned, her voice deep and resonant, echoing with the bitter chill of her resolve. Her eyes, gleaming with malevolence, locked onto Wynter and Seraphis, marking them as the focal points of her vengeance.

With a dramatic flourish of her arms, reminiscent of the icy winds of the fiercest winter storm, she commenced the incantation, each word a venomous barb aimed at the heart of their joy. Her voice, a symphony of darkness, rose and fell with the power of ancient magics, forbidden and feared.

"Ancient powers, heed my call, Bring forth a beast from the depths of thrall. On the night of his eighteenth year, Let this curse become all too clear.

By fire's rage and ice's bite, Transform this prince under the moon's light. Let him see the world through eyes of dread, A monstrous form he shall embody instead.

Only love's true kiss shall break the spell, The torment and despair where he doth dwell. This curse I bind with hate's own seal, On Eirian's soul, let this fate congeal."

As she weaved the curse, spectral chains, shimmering with the light of a thousand lost souls, spiraled through the air, encircling Eirian with the inevitability of fate itself. Her words, a dark miasma, filled the space, leaving a tangible weight of foreboding hanging over the crowd.

The incantation completed, Freya's laughter, a sound as chilling as the deepest winter, cascaded through the courtyard. The ice began to creep over the festivities' remnants, a physical manifestation of the curse's immediate effect, turning joy into despair, warmth into cold fear.

But Freya stood unflinching, her figure cloaked in a swirling mist of her own conjuring. As she laughed, her voice cold and unforgiving, it was as if the very air around her frosted over, sending delicate ripples of ice creeping across the banquet tables and slithering over the dance floors.

"Look upon your queen's work and despair!" she called out, her tone mocking as she observed the pandemonium she had unleashed. The guests, once resplendent in their celebratory attire, now stumbled back, slipping on ice as it formed underfoot, their expressions twisted in fear and uncertainty.

"Seize her!" a guard commanded, drawing closer with a group armed with enchanted spears aimed at her heart.

Yet, with a flick of her wrist, Freya summoned a barrier of ice shards, creating a formidable wall between her and the guards. Their efforts to apprehend her were futile as they grappled with the slippery, treacherous ground, their coordinated movements descending into clumsy chaos.

Amidst this, her laughter continued to echo, a haunting sound that seemed to bounce off the palace walls and into the frosty night air. "Your efforts are as futile as your hopes," she taunted, turning her gaze upon the terrified faces of the kingdom's nobility. "The threads of your fate are woven at my command!"

As the chaos unfolded, Freya made her way slowly back into the shadows from which she had emerged, her steps measured and sure, her heart alight with the fires of vengeance and the thrill of the turmoil she had instigated.

From the epicenter of turmoil she had created, Freya took one final, disdainful glance at Wynter Snow and Seraphis, her eyes alight with the fire of her malevolent intentions. She could feel their despair, their agony, as tangible as the icy air that whipped around her.

"You think you have won," she hissed, her voice cutting through the clamor. "But true power... true power can never be defeated, only displaced." Her words, spoken with the venom of centuries, were aimed to wound, to haunt.

With a final, contemptuous look that promised her vendetta was far from over, Freya invoked one last spell of concealment. "Into the mists of time I recede, but from my curse, you shall never be freed," she whispered, her voice fading as a thick, icy fog enveloped her. When it cleared, she was gone, her departure leaving a void colder than the deepest winter night, a stark reminder of the power and spite that had once ruled—and might yet rule again.

In response, a thick, icy fog billowed outwards, engulfing her in a shroud of ghostly mist. The temperature dropped suddenly, a biting cold that seeped into every corner of the courtyard, sending shivers through everyone gathered.

Wynter and Seraphis reached out towards her, their faces etched with desperation and fury, but their efforts were futile. The fog thickened, becoming an impenetrable wall of ice crystals that glittered under the moonlight.

Then, as quickly as it had appeared, the fog dissipated, melting away into the cool night air. And with it, Freya was gone—vanished without a trace, leaving behind no clue but the chill of her departure and the lingering dread of what her curse might bring.

The crowd was left in stunned silence, the only sounds the soft rustling of leaves and the distant call of a night bird. The ominous reality of the curse laid upon their young prince hung over them like a dark cloud, a reminder of the power and spite of the fallen queen.

The Shadow of the Curse

Beauty

I remember the first time the frost came, how it painted the village in shades of silver and blue. But that fleeting beauty has long since turned to an oppressive chill, the kind that seeps into your bones and settles there, unwelcome and relentless. Eldoria, once a tapestry of green and gold, now lies suffocated under Queen Freya's relentless curse.

The morning greets me with a frigid kiss as I step outside. Icicles hang like daggers from the eaves, sharp and clear against the grey canvas of dawn. Frost-cloaked fields stretch out, a desolate white wasteland under the overcast sky. Villagers shuffle past, their movements sluggish, faces buried in scarves to ward off the biting air.

My heart clenches at the sight—this isn't how life should be. We were meant for sunny days and laughter in the fields, not this eternal winter. Yet as old Mrs. Harkin approaches, her frail body bent like a bow, I can't help but offer her my warmest smile.

"Let me help you with that," I say, reaching for the bundle of firewood she struggles to carry.

"Oh, Beauty," she breaths out a cloud of misty air. "Always so kind."

Her gratitude is a small comfort against the cold that presses in on all sides. As I place the logs by her door, I feel that familiar tug at my heart—the longing for something beyond this frozen existence.

I dream of warmth and sunlight, a world untouched by Freya's icy grasp. And though my hands are numb with cold, inside there's a fire that refuses to die down—a flame fueled by tales of distant lands and hidden magic.

In quiet moments like these, when the village fades into a hushed whisper beneath winter's heavy cloak, I find myself lost in daydreams. There's one in particular that visits me often—a stranger with eyes like twilight skies and secrets as deep as my own.

I shake off the fantasy as I wave goodbye to Mrs. Harkin. Adventure is not for someone like me; there are chores to be done and villagers who rely on my help.

Yet as I gaze out over the horizon, where grey sky meets white earth in an endless kiss, I can't help but wonder what lies beyond those frostbitten fields. Somewhere out there is a life waiting to be lived—a life full of adventure...and perhaps even love.

The curse holds the village in a relentless grip, turning what should be fertile ground into a sheet of unyielding frost. I walk past fields where crops stand like crystal statues, beauty robbed of purpose. The harvests we depend on are now but memories trapped in ice.

"Beauty!" The call pulls me from my reverie. I turn to see Lily, her breath forming clouds in the chill air. She's bundled in layers, but the cold still bites at her exposed cheeks, painting them a rosy hue.

I trudge toward her, noting the hunched figures of villagers behind her. They move with the lethargy of defeat. Children huddle together for warmth, their laughter lost to the winter's silence. A horse whinnies, its breath a steamy protest as it scrapes hooves over frozen earth.

"You're miles away again," Lily chides as I reach her side. "Dreaming won't fill bellies or thaw fields."

Her words sting—a mix of truth and concern. I glance back at the struggling villagers, their resilience etched in lines of worry and frost.

"I know," I murmur, my voice barely more than a whisper carried away by the biting wind. "But if I don't dream, what's left?"

Lily's eyes soften, a glimmer of shared yearning flickering within. "Dreams are luxury we can't afford, Beauty."

I nod, the weight of her words settling on my shoulders like snowflakes—light but accumulating fast.

We walk in silence toward the center of the village where families gather around meager fires that crackle with stubborn life. An old man cradles his hands close to the flames, eyes shut against the harsh reality that surrounds us.

"It isn't fair," I whisper, more to myself than to Lily. The village is my heart; these people are my family. But this life—this half-existence under Freya's cruel hand—it feels like a vise tightening around my future.

"Life seldom is," Lily replies, pulling her shawl tighter around her frame. "We survive—that's what we do."

Her words echo in my chest as I help distribute what little food we have salvaged from the eternal winter's clutches. Yet as I watch a mother wrap her child in layers of tattered blankets, I can't suppress the flicker of defiance that sparks within me.

"Why has no one tried to break it?" I ask suddenly, surprising even myself with the intensity of my question.

Lily glances at me sharply before softening once more. "Because it's bigger than us," she says quietly. "Bigger than our dreams or hopes."

But is it? My gaze drifts again to the horizon, past the ice-bound village to where possibilities might lie beyond this frozen cage. My heart races with unspoken "what ifs," each beat a drumming call to action that I've yet to answer.

"Maybe," I start, then hesitate—aware of Lily's worried gaze upon me—"maybe one day someone will."

As I trudge through the outskirts of the village, the weight of the firewood in my arms is a comforting burden against the relentless chill. The frostbitten trees stand guard like silent sentinels, their branches heavy with snow. It's a lonely place, but solitude has always been a dear friend, whispering secrets the wind carries from distant lands.

My boots crunch through the crust of snow, each step a stubborn defiance against the winter that refuses to release its grip. I pause to catch my breath, steam curling from my lips in wispy tendrils. That's when I see it—a glint of something out of place amidst the white expanse.

Curiosity quickens my pulse as I drop the firewood with a muted thud and kneel beside the oddity. My fingers, red and raw from cold, dig eagerly through the snow. There's a thrill that courses through me, an anticipation for what might lie beneath this frozen veil.

My breath catches in my throat as I brush away the last of the snow, revealing an amulet. It pulses with a soft, golden light, as if it had a heartbeat of its own. The symbols etched upon its surface are foreign yet familiar, dancing before my eyes in an intricate pattern that beckons me closer.

"What is this?" I whisper to myself, cupping the amulet in my hands. "Why do I feel like it's calling to me?" The warmth it radiates seeps into my skin, a stark contrast to the biting cold around me. It's as though the amulet recognizes me—knows me—in ways I can't comprehend.

My mind races with questions, each more urgent than the last. What secrets does this artifact hold? How did it come to be buried here? And why—why does its presence stir something deep within me?

I wrap my fingers around it tightly, afraid that it might vanish if I let go. Afraid that this connection, this strange sense of belonging will disappear like smoke on the wind.

The walk back home feels different somehow. With every step, the amulet against my chest is a constant source of wonder and intrigue. My thoughts swirl with possibilities and whispers of adventure. Could this be the key to unlocking my unspoken dreams?

As I lay down for bed that night, placing the glowing amulet on my bedside table, I can't shake off the feeling that everything is about to change. And deep down, where fear mingles with hope, I'm not sure if I'm ready—but I know there's no turning back now.

The wind howls outside, but within these four walls, a hush falls like a blanket over the world. Here in my modest home, the small fire I've lit flickers with life, its warmth a welcome reprieve from the chill that has become my constant companion. I sit cross-legged on the worn rug, the amulet lying before me, an enigma wrapped in gold.

I lean closer, the light from the fire casting dancing shadows across its surface. My fingers tremble as they trace the symbols etched into the metal—strange runes that feel both alien and achingly familiar. I squint, concentrating on each curve and line, willing them to make sense.

A surge of energy courses through me as one by one, the symbols begin to unravel their secrets. They speak of fire and flight, of scales that shimmer like jewels under the sun. They whisper of a lineage steeped in magic—a lineage that flows through my veins.

The realization hits me like a thunderclap: dragon shifters. Beings of legend and power, capable of tearing through skies and commanding the elements. And somehow, impossibly, I am one of them.

My breath catches in my throat—a dragon shifter? Me? How could I not have known? How could this vital piece of who I am have remained hidden for so long? My life has been nothing but mundane tasks and simple pleasures; there's been no hint of flame or flight in my blood—until now.

The artifact pulses brighter, its glow illuminating the room with a golden hue that seems to breathe life into every shadow. It feels alive, resonating with a part of me I've never known. The room shrinks away as if giving space to the enormity of what this means.

Excitement flutters in my chest like a caged bird eager for release. Adventure beckons—a call to embrace this newfound heritage and soar beyond the confines of this cursed winter. But fear grips me just as tightly; fear of the unknown, fear of a power that could consume me if left unchecked.

"Could this be real?" The words slip from my lips in a hushed awe. The amulet doesn't answer with words but responds with a warmth that seeps into my core—a silent affirmation that yes, this is real; yes, you are part of something greater.

My eyes scan the markings again—now clear as if they've always been meant for me. They tell a tale of the last heir to an ancient throne, an heir with fire in her heart and wings waiting to unfurl. My hands shake as I hold the amulet up to the light.

This is more than I ever dared to dream—more wondrous and more terrifying than anything I've known. A new path unfolds before me—one fraught with peril but also brimming with promise.

The amulet's light beats in sync with my heart—a steady drum heralding change. It's a bond sealed in magic and mystery, one that tugs at me with an urgency that demands attention.

Here by the fire's glow, wrapped in solitude and silence save for the crackle of flames, destiny whispers my name. And despite everything—the doubts that nip at my heels like winter's chill—I find myself leaning into its call.

The amulet's glow casts an otherworldly light across the room, its radiance touching each shadowed corner like a promise. My hands tremble as I cradle it, feeling the weight of a thousand generations in my palm. A decision looms before me, monumental and terrifying. Do I heed its call, or do I remain here, shackled by duty and fear?

"If I stay, I'll never know who I truly am," I whisper to the walls that have known me since childhood. "But what if I fail?" The questions swirl in my mind, each one a weight on my heart.

A soft knock interrupts my thoughts. "Beauty?" Lily's voice seeps through the wood, tinged with concern.

I open the door to find her standing there, a lifeline thrown into the turbulent sea of my doubts. "Lily," I start, the word a lifeline in itself.

She steps inside, her gaze immediately drawn to the amulet in my hands. "What's that?"

With hesitant fingers, I extend the artifact toward her. Her eyes widen with a mix of awe and concern as she examines it. "This... This is what's been calling to me."

Lily reaches out to touch the glowing symbols but pulls back at the last moment. "It's beautiful," she breathes out.

I nod, a flurry of emotions battling within me. "It's more than that. It's a clue to who I am...to my heritage."

We sit on the edge of my bed, the amulet between us like a shared secret. Lily listens intently as I confess my fears and hopes. "I'm torn," I admit. "My place is here, but so is this pull toward something greater."

"You've always dreamed of something more," Lily says softly, her hand finding mine in comfort. "Maybe this is your chance." Her words are a balm to my troubled mind.

A long silence stretches between us before she adds, "The village will survive, Beauty. We always have." There's an undeniable strength in her voice—a conviction that fuels my wavering courage.

I let out a breath I didn't realize I'd been holding. "Lily believes in me," I think to myself. "Maybe I can do this."

The night whispers through slightly ajar windows as I pack a small bag with essentials—food, clothing, and the amulet nestled safely at its heart. The cold air bites at my skin when I step outside, but it cannot quench the fire that blazes within me now.

With each step away from my home, fear and excitement dance together in my chest. The amulet's glow warms against me—a silent encouragement—as if it knows this is just the beginning.

"This is the start of something big," I murmur into the darkness. A final glance back at my village etches its familiar silhouette into memory—one last image before turning toward adventure.

The path ahead is shrouded in mystery; every shadow holds potential peril or promise. But with each stride forward, guided by the golden light that seems to pulse in time with my heartbeat, one thought rings clear and true: "I'm ready."

The Dragon's Heart

Beauty

I sat there, in the quiet of my small room, the amulet's soft glow bathing my face in light. The only other source of illumination was a single candle, its flame dancing to an unheard melody, casting shadows that played like silent music on the walls. I couldn't shake off the feeling that those flickering shapes knew more about my fate than I did.

My fingers trembled slightly as I reached out to touch the amulet. The surface was warm against my skin, warmer than anything should be in this unending winter. It was as if the artifact carried its own heartbeat, a pulse of life that defied the cold grasp of Freya's curse.

"What could these symbols mean?" I whispered to myself, my voice barely audible above the crackle of the candle. "Could they really be connected to me?" The etchings were foreign yet familiar, like a song I had once known but forgotten. The amulet felt like a key waiting to unlock parts of myself I never knew existed.

As I traced each intricate symbol, a sense of wonder washed over me. This was more than just an artifact; it was a part of my heritage. With every line and curve that my fingertips caressed, I felt a step closer to unraveling the mystery of my lineage—of who and what I truly was.

The room seemed to grow colder as I delved deeper into the enigma of the amulet, but its warmth never waned. It was as though it whispered secrets just for me, secrets that had been guarded for generations. My heart pounded with anticipation and a touch of fear; what would it mean to fully embrace this legacy?

The Dragon Heart—it had to be. The name resonated within me like a call to arms. The stories said it held immense power, power enough to change the very fabric of our world. And it was here with me, waiting, urging me on.

My eyes widened with each symbol I deciphered—a language of dragons that seemed to speak directly to my soul. Fear mingled with excitement as the reality set in: this journey would transform everything I knew about myself and about Eldoria.

I drew in a deep breath, steadying my nerves. "What secrets do you hold?" I murmured to the glowing heart in my hands. "Could you really be the key to my destiny?" There was no turning back now; this path was mine to walk. And so, with the Dragon Heart's warmth seeping into my very bones, I resolved to step into the unknown and claim the heritage that awaited me.

As I traced the last symbol, the amulet flared to life, its glow intensifying until it bathed the entire room in a soft, golden light. A gentle click echoed through the silence, and I watched in awe as a compartment I hadn't noticed before eased open. Inside lay a scroll, its edges worn by time, yet the parchment itself seemed to thrum with vitality.

I reached out with hesitant fingers, my heart a fluttering bird trapped within my chest. The thrill of discovery raced through my veins even as fear nipped at its heels. What secrets did this ancient relic hold? With a breath I didn't realize I'd been holding, I unfurled the scroll.

The words were written in an elegant script that shimmered like moonlight on water. They pulsed as if alive, resonating with an energy that seemed to call out to something dormant within me. My eyes devoured the text, and with each word, a thunderbolt of realization struck deep into my core.

"I am a dragon shifter?" The words tumbled from my lips in a hushed whisper of disbelief. How could this be? My entire life had been nothing but ordinary—mundane even. And yet here was proof of a heritage grander and more ancient than any story told around the fireside.

What does it mean for my future and my place in this world? The weight of the revelation bore down on me, heavy with responsibility and brimming with questions that begged for answers. This was not just about who I was but who I was meant to become.

A surge of power coursed through me as I clutched the scroll closer, its warmth seeping into my bones like the first rays of dawn after a long night. Destiny was calling me, whispering promises of strength and purpose I had never dared to dream of.

The room seemed to embrace me then, growing warmer as if acknowledging the awakening of my true nature. The artifact's glow became a beacon, reflecting not only the light but also the burgeoning power within me—a power that was mine by birthright.

"A dragon shifter... me?" My voice broke the stillness again, this time laced with wonder and an inkling of pride. What does this mean for my future, for my place in the world? As daunting as these questions were, they also ignited a spark of excitement—an ember that threatened to blaze into an inferno of determination.

I knew then that nothing would ever be the same again. With trembling hands but a steadfast heart, I resolved to step into this new chapter of my life—one where I would embrace my lineage and rise to meet whatever challenges lay ahead. This was more than just an artifact or a scroll; it was an invitation to claim my destiny as the last heir of an ancient line of dragon shifters. And I would answer that call.

A tempest of emotion churned within me as I paced the confines of my modest chamber, the ancient scroll clutched in my trembling hands. My breath came in shallow bursts, a testament to the whirlwind of fear and exhilaration that battled for dominance in my heart. How does one grapple with the revelation of being the last of a lineage so steeped in legend that it seemed more myth than reality?

The weight of my newfound identity bore down on me with an almost physical force, each step I took a labored trudge through the snowdrifts of uncertainty. How do I even begin to embrace this heritage? The thought echoed in my mind, a relentless drumbeat that fueled my restless energy.

My reflection caught my eye in the small mirror perched atop my dresser. The same blue eyes stared back at me, wide with a mix of wonder and trepidation. The same unassuming features that had always been mine gazed back, unchanged. And yet, everything was different now. There was no outward sign of the dragon shifter that supposedly resided within me, no hint of scales or fire beneath my skin. But the scroll's words had awakened something—a flicker of power that whispered promises of transformation.

I stopped pacing and faced my reflection squarely, as if challenging it to reveal its secrets. "What if I fail?" The question slipped out, voicing the fear that gripped me. To fail would mean to remain trapped in this life of quiet desperation, never knowing what could have been.

But then another thought rose, bright and defiant against the shadows of doubt. "But what if I succeed and can change everything for my village and myself?" That possibility sparked a flame within me, a beacon against the encroaching dark. To embrace my heritage could mean salvation for those I loved, a chance to lift Freya's curse and bring back the warmth of spring.

I drew a deep breath, steadying myself against the tide of emotions. With each exhalation, I felt a sliver of calm return. My hands no longer shook as I rolled up the scroll with deliberate care. The decision lay before me like the path through an uncharted forest—daunting, yes, but filled with the potential for wonders untold.

I knew then that I could not—would not—let fear dictate my course. The legacy of dragon shifters was mine to claim, and with it, the power to forge a new destiny not just for myself but for all of Eldoria.

Resolved, I tucked the scroll into my belt and turned away from the mirror. My journey was only just beginning, and though I did not know what trials awaited me, I would meet them head-on. For within me burned the heart of a dragon, and it was time to let it soar.

I pulled my cloak tighter around my shoulders, the chill of the evening seeping into my bones as I made my way through the hushed streets of our village. The snow crunched underfoot, a constant reminder of the curse that held us all in its icy grasp. I sought out the quiet corner where I knew Lily would be waiting, the weight of the secret I carried pressing down on me with each step.

As I rounded the corner, I spotted her silhouette, wrapped in her own cloak, her breath forming misty clouds in the cold air. My heart hammered against my ribs, a mix of fear and hope fluttering within me like a caged bird desperate for release.

"Lily," I began, my voice barely above a whisper as she turned to face me. "I found something... something incredible and terrifying. I think I might be a dragon shifter."

Her eyes widened, reflecting the pale moonlight, and for a moment, all was silent save for the whispering wind. I braced myself for disbelief, for laughter, for rejection. But none came.

Instead, Lily stepped forward, her expression etched with amazement and concern. "Beauty," she breathed, reaching out to steady me as my knees threatened to buckle under the enormity of what I had confessed. "This is incredible. You have to embrace it. I believe in you."

Her words were a lifeline thrown across the chasm of my doubts. Lily believes in me. Maybe I can do this. I have to try.

I felt the tightness in my chest ease slightly as she pulled me into an embrace, her warmth seeping into my chilled bones. We stood there for a long moment, two friends bound by a secret that would change everything.

"Lily," I said again as we stepped back from each other, "what if it's true? What if I can... what if I can shift?"

"Then we'll figure it out together," she replied with a determination that bolstered my flagging spirits. "You're not alone in this, Beauty."

Her unwavering support was like a beacon in the darkness that had begun to envelop my heart. With Lily by my side, perhaps there was hope yet—not just for me but for our entire village.

The bond between us deepened in that quiet corner of Eldoria as we shared this intimate moment of revelation and acceptance. With Lily's belief fueling my resolve, I knew that whatever lay ahead on this strange and wondrous path, I would not face it alone.

With a resolve that surprised even myself, I decided to embrace the truth of my heritage. It was as if the amulet around my neck pulsed with approval, its warm glow a silent encouragement. "I must seek out more information about my lineage and powers," I whispered to the walls of my small room, the only witness to my monumental decision.

Determination surged through me, mingling with a courage I hadn't known I possessed. The prospect of stepping beyond the boundaries of my village—my entire world up to this moment—filled me with a sense of purpose that was as invigorating as it was terrifying.

I pulled my weathered pack from beneath my bed, dust motes dancing in the sliver of moonlight that crept through the window. My hands were steady as I placed the essentials inside: a loaf of bread, a flask of water, and my thickest cloak against the chill that never seemed to leave Eldoria. Then, with a reverence that made my hands tremble, I laid the artifact and the scroll on top. They were more than mere objects; they were keys to a past shrouded in mystery and a future ripe with possibility.

"This is it," I murmured, securing the clasp on my pack. "I need to find out who I truly am and what I'm capable of." The walls offered no response, but in their silence, I found affirmation. I couldn't stay here any longer—not when every fiber of my being urged me forward.

My heart hammered against my ribcage as if echoing the drumbeat of destiny itself. Fear mingled with excitement—a potent cocktail that sharpened my senses and lent lightness to my step. As I shouldered my pack and reached for the door, the amulet glowed brighter still, casting a halo of light that seemed to beckon me onward.

I took a deep breath, letting it out slowly to quell the fluttering in my stomach. With each exhale, apprehension gave way to anticipation.

"Determination fills me," I affirmed, steeling myself for the journey ahead. "A newfound sense of purpose and direction. I will embrace my destiny, no matter the cost."

The door creaked open, revealing a world cloaked in silver frost—a world waiting for its thaw. As I crossed the threshold into the unknown, one thought rose above all others: "I need to find out who I truly am and what I'm capable of."

And with that single thought propelling me forward into the night's embrace, there was no turning back.

I slipped through the shadows, my feet treading softly on the snow-covered path. The village lay shrouded in a blanket of silence, its slumbering forms oblivious to the solitary figure stealing away under the cloak of night. A frigid breeze danced through the empty streets, nipping at my exposed skin with its frosty teeth. But nestled against my chest, beneath layers of wool and leather, the amulet pulsed with a gentle warmth that kept the cold at bay.

The luminous glow from the artifact cast an otherworldly light on my path, a beacon amidst the darkness that surrounded me. It was a silent guide, its radiance a stark contrast to the dimmed hearths of my neighbors' homes. With each step I took, the light seemed to grow stronger, as if encouraging me to press on, to embrace this journey that lay ahead.

A swirl of emotions churned within me—a potent cocktail of fear for what dangers might lurk beyond, excitement for the adventure that beckoned, and an underlying current of sadness for what I was leaving behind. My heart ached with the knowledge that when—or if—I returned, nothing would be as it once was. I was changing, transforming in ways I could scarcely comprehend.

I paused at the edge of Eldoria, where civilization gave way to the wilds beyond. The village's familiar thatched roofs and smoking chimneys stood stark against the night sky. My breath caught in my throat as I allowed myself one final glance back at the only home I'd ever known.

"Goodbye, home," I whispered into the stillness. "I hope I can come back one day with the power to change our fate."

The cold night air bit at my skin as I turned away from Eldoria, but inside me burned a flame that no winter could extinguish—the flame of hope and determination. Each step forward felt like a declaration, a vow to myself and to those I loved that I would not let Freya's curse condemn us to an eternity of frost and sorrow.

I felt the weight of my decision settle upon my shoulders with every crunch of snow beneath my boots. This was no longer just about me; it was about all of us—every soul who had suffered under this endless winter.

With a deep breath that sent plumes of vapor spiraling into the air, I steeled myself for what lay ahead. The artifact's glow illuminated my way as I ventured into the unknown, my heart steadfast and full of resolve.

"Each step away from the village is a step towards my destiny," I promised myself. And with that vow echoing in my heart, I stepped into the wilderness, leaving behind everything familiar—and stepping into legend.

The forest swallowed me whole, its towering trees casting long, gnarled shadows that seemed to reach for me with skeletal fingers. I pressed on, the amulet's glow my steadfast companion in the darkening woods. It was then I noticed the figure, a mere wisp of darkness within the cloak of night, standing so still it could have been mistaken for another tree—if not for the faint glimmer of light reflecting off their eyes.

"Who are you? Why are you here?" My voice was steady, a testament to my resolve despite the rapid drumming of my heart against my ribs.

The figure stepped forward, emerging from the veil of shadows into the dim light cast by my amulet. The cloak they wore did little to reveal their identity, but there was an undeniable gentleness in their stance, a powerful presence that seemed to echo with the whisper of ancient woods.

"I am here to help you find your true path," they replied, their voice as soft as falling snow yet carrying an authority that commanded the night's attention.

Can I trust this stranger? Do they truly know what I seek? My mind raced with questions, yet somewhere deep within, a sense of connection tugged at my soul—a silent acknowledgment that our meeting was more than mere chance.

I studied them for a moment longer, searching for any sign of deceit. But there was none; only an inscrutable calm that seemed as old as the forest itself. The amulet warmed against my skin, as if urging me on, whispering of destiny and paths yet walked.

"You know of my quest?" I ventured cautiously.

"I know of many things," they said, stepping closer still. "But most importantly, I know of you, Beauty—the last heir of the dragon shifters."

A shiver ran down my spine at the mention of my name. How could this stranger know who I was when I had only just begun to understand myself?

"I will guide you to where your journey must continue," they offered, extending a hand cloaked in shadow. "But know this: the path will not be easy, and what you seek may change you in ways unimaginable."

Their words hung heavy in the air, laden with truths I wasn't sure I was ready to face. Yet hesitation was a luxury I could ill afford. With a deep breath that steadied my nerves and fortified my resolve, I placed my hand in theirs—a silent pact sealed beneath the watchful eyes of ancient trees.

"I'm searching for the Beast, someone who is both more and less than he seems.," I admitted, meeting their gaze with determination. "Someone who can help me break the curse on my village."

The figure nodded, a knowing glint in their eyes. "Then let us find it together," they said, their voice a promise of guidance and solidarity.

"Lead on," I said, and together we stepped deeper into the heart of the forest—a place where light and darkness danced in an eternal embrace and where my fate awaited, shrouded in mystery and intrigue.

The Cursed Prince

Prince Eirian, the Dragon Beast

The castle loomed like a forsaken sentinel atop the craggy peak, its cold stone walls cloaked in shadows, the once-grand halls now echoing with the whispers of lost hope. In my dragon form, I paced the length of the great hall, each heavy step resounding off the walls, a stark reminder of my solitude.

My claws traced the rough stone of the corridor, a futile attempt to find comfort in the familiarity of my prison. I could almost feel the warmth of the hearth fires that had once blazed here, now extinguished and replaced by a chill that seemed to emanate from within me.

This castle is my tomb, and I, its eternal prisoner. Will I ever break free of this darkness? The question haunted me as much as the spectral wind that moaned through the broken battlements.

Once, laughter and life had filled these halls—a time before Freya's curse had twisted my fate into this grotesque parody of existence. My noble visage marred by scales and fangs, my honor-bound spirit caged within a beast's hideous form. How cruelly ironic that she chose to make a monster out of a prince who sought only to serve his people.

In the depths of night, I would often retreat to my private chambers, shedding my dragon skin for the fleeting comfort of humanity. Here, in this dimly lit refuge, I dared to reminisce about days long gone—days of sunlight and smiles. But even as a man, I could not escape the beast that lurked beneath the surface. It clawed at my conscience with sharp reminders of all I had lost.

A mirror stood against one wall—a cruel jest left behind by some forgotten servant. I avoided its reflective surface; it only offered glimpses of a stranger wearing my crown. The eyes staring back held a glimmer of something fierce and untamed—a beast waiting to break free.

Sometimes, in moments when despair grew too heavy a burden, I allowed myself to hope. Perhaps one day someone would see past this cursed exterior to the man trapped within—someone who could look into these eyes and recognize the soul they concealed.

Yet hope was as treacherous as it was comforting. It whispered sweet lies of salvation and love—concepts alien to one such as I. Who could love a dragon? Who could love a beast?

Silent tears would fall—tears not fit for dragon eyes—as I succumbed to dreams of redemption. But dawn always brought back harsh reality with its unforgiving light.

I roared into the emptiness—a dragon's cry that shook the very foundations of my stronghold—venting fury and anguish into the uncaring void. But no one answered; no one ever did.

As morning light crept through the cracks in the stone, casting pale rays onto the dusty floor, I faced another day alone—alone with my curse, alone with my regrets. And yet, amidst it all, there lingered a stubborn spark—a spark that refused to be extinguished.

For even in this darkened state, I could not relinquish all hope. Perhaps it was pride or merely human folly that spurred me on. But whatever it was, it held me captive more securely than any curse ever could.

That opulent hall of my sixteenth birthday, once a haven of light and laughter, transformed into a theater of shadows and foreboding under the weight of Freya's curse. The very air seemed to thicken with dark anticipation as she stepped forward, her eyes gleaming with a malice that made my blood run cold.

"Why, Freya?" I managed to choke out, my voice barely carrying over the sudden silence that had befallen the crowd. Her smile was a dagger to my heart, the edge of betrayal sharper than any blade.

"Because, dear Eirian," she began, her voice smooth as the surface of a frozen lake, "you represent everything I have been denied. Your happiness is an affront to the throne I was meant to claim." The air crackled with her rising power, a storm unleashed by words alone.

As she spoke the incantation, spectral chains spiraled around me, their links forged from the depths of her hatred. I could feel them tightening, constricting, as if they sought to crush the very hope from my chest. The pain was immediate and searing; it spread through my limbs like wildfire, contorting my body into something grotesque and unrecognizable.

The transformation took place on my eighteenth birthday. It was agony incarnate. Each bone in my body splintered and reformed, muscles bulging and skin stretching over scales that emerged like dark jewels from beneath. My screams seemed to be mingled with Freya's triumphant laughter, echoing off the stone walls until they became indistinguishable—a chorus of despair.

In the present moment, my fists clenched involuntarily as the memory gnawed at me. Claws sank into flesh, a stark reminder of the beast I had become. My heart still bore the scars of that night—scars that ran deeper than the scales on my skin.

As I sat alone in the shadowy confines of what had become my sanctuary and prison all at once, I couldn't help but wonder if there was more to her curse than mere vengeance. Was there a lesson hidden within this cruel fate? A test of character or strength?

With each passing day, I grew more determined to unravel the threads of Freya's spell—to find redemption not only for myself but for a kingdom caught in the crossfire of our strife. The weight of her curse bore down on me with every breath I took in this monstrous form.

Yet hope is a stubborn flame; it flickers even in the darkest night. And so I hold onto it—onto the possibility that love might indeed be powerful enough to break this curse and restore not just my humanity but peace to Eldoria once more.

Surrounded by the dusty tomes and faded scrolls of my study, I delved into ancient curses and their counters with a fervor born of desperation. My claws scraped against parchment, a grating sound that had become all too familiar in the echoing silence of my isolation. Yet no matter how deep I searched, the answers seemed to slip through my grasp like smoke.

That's when it happened—a warmth seeped into the air, a gentle caress against the chill that had long claimed Arvendon Castle as its own. I stilled, every muscle tensed, my breath caught in my throat. This was not the biting frost of Freya's magic; this was something else entirely.

"What is this feeling?" The words fell from my lips, a whisper of sound that seemed to tremble with the stirrings of hope. I stood abruptly, my chair clattering to the stone floor behind me. The frost-covered windowpane before me held no answers, but I could not tear my gaze away.

The sensation was alien—like the first tentative rays of dawn after an endless night. It pulsed through me, an ember that dared to glow amidst the suffocating darkness of my curse. Could it be that after all these years of solitude and sorrow, a glimmer of light had found its way to me?

"This presence... it's unlike anything I've felt in years." Doubt gnawed at the edges of my cautious optimism. Was it merely a trick of my weary mind? A cruel jest from some mischievous spirit? Or perhaps...

No. I dared not entertain the thought too deeply. To hope was to open myself to disappointment once more, and yet... "Could it be someone who can help me? Or another cruel trick?" My voice broke the silence again, sounding foreign even to my own ears—tinged with a vulnerability I'd long since buried beneath layers of cynicism.

With hesitant steps, I approached the window, my hand reaching out to touch the glass before pulling back. The cold bite of ice met my fingertips briefly before giving way to that inexplicable warmth. It beckoned me, whispered promises that I feared to believe.

"This presence..." My heart hammered within my chest as if awakening from a long slumber. "Dare I hope it's someone who can help me?" The question hung in the air, mingling with the dust motes that danced in the stray shafts of moonlight.

I could not ignore this call, this faint echo of possibility that stirred something within me that had lain dormant for far too long—the ember of hope, fragile and precious. With a deep breath to steady myself, I resolved to investigate this disturbance. Whatever it may bring, for good or ill, I could not remain ensconced within these walls any longer—not when chance had cast its lot at my feet.

Drawing upon the strength that had sustained me through countless nights of despair, I donned my cloak and made for the door. The castle loomed large around me as I moved through its corridors—a beast within its lair—and yet tonight, it felt less like a prison and more like a starting point from which something new might begin.

The mist hung heavy around the outskirts of my domain, a veil that whispered secrets to those who dared to listen. It was within this shroud that I first beheld her—a silhouette against the pallid moonlight, the amulet in her grasp casting a soft luminescence that seemed to pierce the fog. I stilled, a primal instinct warning me of the danger in revealing myself, yet an inexplicable force urged me forward.

I watched, transfixed, as she stepped with cautious grace, her eyes wide with wonder and trepidation. The amulet's glow bathed her in a light that seemed not of this cursed realm—a beacon that called to something long dormant within me. Fear of rejection clawed at my chest, a familiar specter that had kept me secluded within these stone walls for too long. What would she see when she looked upon me? A monster? A beast of nightmares?

My talons dug into the damp earth as I wrestled with the desire to approach her. To connect with another soul after so much solitude was a temptation I could scarcely resist. Yet, the fear of scaring her away, of seeing that same revulsion I had seen mirrored in so many eyes before, held me captive.

I took a step closer, emerging from the shadow of an ancient oak. My form was half-concealed by the mist—enough to obscure my monstrous visage but not enough to go unnoticed. She turned sharply at the sound of my movement, and our eyes met for a fleeting moment. Her gasp sliced through the silence like a blade, and yet she did not flee.

"She's not running away," I murmured under my breath, disbelief coloring my tone. "Why isn't she running?" My heart hammered against my ribcage with such ferocity that it threatened to break free. Could she be the one? The one who could see past this accursed form—to see me?

The tension between us was a living thing, coiling around us like the very mist that shrouded my cursed existence. Her gaze held mine—a myriad of emotions swirling within those depths: fear, curiosity... and something else I dared not name.

With each second that passed in which she did not turn away from me, hope flickered in my chest like a candle fighting against the darkness. The urge to step closer grew stronger until it was all-consuming. "Who are you?" I wanted to ask. "Why have you come here?"

But no words passed my lips as I cautiously approached her, each step measured and deliberate. The beast within urged me to retreat into the shadows—to spare myself potential heartache—but I could not. Not now.

She stood her ground, her hands clutching the amulet as if it were a lifeline. Her bravery was a thing of beauty in itself—a stark contrast to the life of fear and isolation I had led.

And so we remained, locked in a moment of silent understanding—a beast and a beauty who had stumbled upon each other at the crossroads of fate and despair. What this encounter would bring, only time would tell. But for now, I let myself bask in the simple wonder of her presence—the closest thing to warmth I had felt in an age.

I stood before her, the air thick with a tension that felt almost tangible. Mist swirled at our feet, like a dance of apprehension and intrigue. Her eyes, wide with a courage that seemed to defy the very nature of her situation, met mine. In her grip, the amulet glowed—a beacon in the oppressive gloom of my existence.

"Who are you?" Her voice trembled slightly, but the determination behind it was clear and steadfast.

I grappled with an urge to retreat into the shadows from whence I came, to spare us both the cruelty of this encounter. But something about her—the strength she emanated—held me rooted to the spot.

"I should ask you the same," I responded, my voice rough as gravel, betraying none of the tempest that raged within me. My form loomed over her, a dark specter veiled in mist and doubt.

"Why are you here?" she pressed on, her grip on the amulet tightening as if it could shield her from whatever threat I might pose.

I circled her slowly, my gaze never wavering from hers. "I guard these lands," I said, every word laced with a defensive edge I could not soften. "And you've ventured far from safety."

Her eyes narrowed slightly, a spark of curiosity igniting within them. "And what if I'm searching for something... someone who can help my village?"

The sheer audacity of her quest struck a chord within me. Could she be speaking of my curse? Of me? My heart dared to skip a beat at the thought. "And who is it you seek?"

"A beast," she replied, "one who is both more and less than he seems."

A growl rumbled in my chest—an involuntary reaction to the title that had been both my condemnation and my shield. Yet there was no disgust in her tone, only a sense of purpose that I found myself envying.

"I am he," I admitted with a guarded caution that had become second nature. My form shifted uneasily, betraying an inner turmoil that belied my imposing stature.

Her eyes searched mine, and for a moment, I felt as if she could see straight through to the soul I feared had long since withered away. "Can you help us? Can you end this winter?"

Her question hung between us—a challenge and a plea wrapped into one. Could I trust her? Dare I even consider it? My mind raced with doubts and fragile hopes.

"Perhaps," I conceded warily. "But why would you seek such a creature? Why place your faith in a beast?"

She stepped closer then—a bold move that made my breath catch in my throat. "Because sometimes," she said softly but with an unwavering conviction that resonated deep within me, "even beasts can be heroes."

In those words lay an echo of possibility—a hint of redemption that seemed both terrifying and tantalizing all at once. Could she be the key to breaking this curse? Could someone like me even be worthy of such salvation?

As we stood there—beast and beauty—I found myself caught in the grip of an emotion I had not dared to entertain for far too long: hope.

The cold mist that enveloped us was a shroud I knew all too well—the same one that had cloaked my heart in ice since the day the curse befell me. As Beauty's inquisitive gaze held mine, memories of a life once lived, a life before the curse, began to surface from the depths of my soul. The castle halls echoed with the laughter of my past self, a man unmarked by the beast's shadow. There were feasts and celebrations, the warmth of family ties, and the admiration of those who called me their prince.

"Can I ever go back to being that person?" I wondered aloud, my voice barely more than a whisper carried away by the wind. The weight of unworthiness bore down upon me like the mountains that bordered my cursed domain. "Would she even want to help me if she knew the truth?"

The truth of what I had become—a creature feared and shunned—clawed at me from within. But as I stood before her, this woman whose bravery seemed to defy the realm of possibility, I felt a flicker of something long forgotten. Was it hope? Or perhaps the warmth of connection that had been absent from my life for so long?

I found myself taking an unsteady breath, as if testing the air after a century beneath the waves. "Before... before this," I gestured vaguely at my scaled form, "I was different. There was light in my life, and joy." The words felt foreign on my tongue, like recalling a language not spoken in ages.

Her eyes softened at my confession, and it was then that I saw it—the look that was neither fear nor disgust but something akin to understanding. It stirred something within me, something vulnerable and raw.

"I want to help you," she said earnestly, stepping closer yet again—a move that sent ripples through the mist and through my being.

My instinct was to recoil, to hide away from her offered kindness. But instead, I found myself yearning to lean into it—to bask in this unfamiliar glow she brought with her.

"Maybe," I dared to hope as her hand reached out tentatively towards mine, "maybe she can see beyond the beast. Maybe she can help me find redemption."

I hesitated for a heartbeat before allowing our hands to touch—a fleeting contact that held more promise than I could have imagined. It was a beginning—tentative and fragile—but a beginning nonetheless.

And as we stood there, surrounded by a world caught between ice and shadow, I allowed myself to believe in the possibility of change—for my cursed land and for my even more cursed heart.

As we stood at the edge of my domain, where the earth kissed the creeping mists, a silent agreement passed between us. Beauty's gaze held mine, steadfast and unyielding, and in that moment, I knew she was my ally in this quest—my only ally.

"This is it," I murmured, the words slipping out like a sacred vow. "My chance for redemption, for breaking the curse. And she's willing to help me. I mustn't fail."

Her nod was subtle, yet it carried the weight of kingdoms. "We will find the a way to end this curse," she declared with a conviction that seemed to pierce through the veil of my endless winter.

The mist around us swirled like ghostly dancers as we agreed to join forces. There was no grand declaration, no shaking of hands—just a shared resolve that felt as old as the land itself. I couldn't help but wonder at this turn of fate. After years of isolation, after resigning myself to an eternity of solitude and despair, here stood someone willing to stand beside me.

I felt it then—a cautious thread of hope weaving through the fabric of my being. It was fragile yet persistent, daring me to believe that perhaps there was still a place for me in this world—a world that had long since turned its back on me.

We took our first steps together into the unknown, the amulet in her grasp casting an ethereal glow that cut through the darkness like a beacon. Our shadows stretched out behind us, long and distorted, as if reluctant to let us go.

I could sense her determination radiating like warmth from a hearth I had not been near for countless moons. And yet, there was vulnerability there too—a mirror of my own. For all her strength and courage, Beauty was stepping into a tale woven with danger and uncertainty just as much as I.

"Together, we might just stand a chance," I found myself thinking aloud. "But what will she think of me once she knows the full truth?"

Her eyes met mine again, and something unspoken passed between us—a flicker of understanding that hinted at a bond deeper than either of us could have anticipated.

As we traversed the boundary of my cursed existence, leaving behind the realm I had both ruled and been imprisoned by, I dared to let that flicker grow. With each step forward, anticipation twined with fear in my chest—a symphony of emotions I had not allowed myself to feel in an age.

We did not speak much as we ventured forth; words seemed trivial amidst the gravity of our undertaking. Yet in that silence grew a kinship that needed no language—a kinship born of shared purpose and a burgeoning trust.

And so we journeyed onward, two souls cast adrift on tides of magic and mystery—seeking an artifact that held the power to alter our destinies forever.

The Call to Adventure

Beauty

The icy forest stood as a bleak, desolate wasteland. What little light filtered through the gnarled, barren branches only seemed to leach what little warmth remained from the world. Everything was shrouded in shades of dull gray and lifeless white, as if the landscape itself had been frozen in time and abandoned to the cruelties of winter's wrath.

Frost clung to every surface in jagged, clinging layers. The clearing where I stood was blanketed in snow, each step muffled by the powdery drifts that erased all signs of life. No birds called, no animals stirred - only an oppressive silence permeated the frigid air.

Determination surged within me like a river breaking through an ice dam. My heart pounded with the weight of what was at stake. "We can't wait any longer," I said, my voice steady despite the quiver of excitement that threatened to betray my nerves. "We have to act now."

Eirian's gaze met mine, and I could see the storm of emotions churning in his eyes—the war between hope and fear, longing and despair. But beneath it all, there flickered a spark that might have been hope.

"This is our chance to change everything," I continued, stepping closer to him. The Dragon's Heart hung heavy around my neck, its glow a beacon in the dawning light. "With this amulet, we can find a way to lift your curse and the frozen grip of Freya. Together."

He shifted uneasily, his clawed feet digging into the earth as if grappling with the very roots of his hesitation. I knew that for Eirian, trust did not come easily—not when betrayal had cost him so much.

"Dawn brings new beginnings," I whispered, not just for him but for myself as well. "Let us be the architects of our fate rather than its prisoners."

His silence was an ocean of thought in which I saw my reflection—a girl who had stumbled upon her destiny in the snow-covered remains of her cursed village. A girl who now stood before a dragon prince as an equal.

The rising sun painted streaks of crimson and gold across his scales, setting them ablaze with light that seemed to dance and flicker with life. It was as if nature itself was urging us on, willing us to seize this fleeting moment before it slipped like sand through our fingers.

I reached out tentatively and placed my hand against his chest—a gesture both bold and gentle. "Eirian," I said softly, my voice imbued with all the courage I could muster, "let us reclaim what has been taken from us."

And in that moment, as he looked down at me with eyes that mirrored the tumultuous skies of his homeland—clouded yet capable of such clarity—I knew we would embark on this journey together. For it was not just about breaking curses or reclaiming thrones; it was about discovering who we truly were beneath the layers of fear and magic that cloaked us.

"We will find a way," he finally said, his voice resonant with a resolve that matched my own. And with those words spoken into the dawn's embrace, our pact was sealed.

Eirian's towering form cast a long shadow that melded with the trees, the frozen stillness of the forest amplifying the weight of our shared silence. His expression was conflicted, as if every word I had spoken wrestled with the doubts lurking within him. I could almost hear his thoughts churning like a tempest against the shores of his resolve.

"What if we fail?" His voice broke the hush, a low rumble that seemed to resonate with the very earth beneath our feet. "What if this only leads to more pain?"

I felt a pang of empathy pierce through me. I knew his fear, for it echoed my own—a haunting refrain that threatened to unseat my newfound courage. But as I watched him, the morning light casting an ethereal glow upon his scaled visage, I saw not just a cursed prince but a kindred spirit.

"The prospect of our quest excites me," he continued, his gaze distant, "but the fear of failure... it's a heavy chain." His brow furrowed, and I saw in his eyes the reflection of a soul torn between hope and despair.

I stepped closer, my own shadow merging with his. "Eirian," I said softly, my voice steady despite the quickening of my heart. "I too am afraid. But we cannot let fear dictate our fate."

The icy landscape around us was quiet, almost reverent, as if nature itself held its breath awaiting his response. The weight of our decision pressed upon us, heavy as the icicles hanging on the branches.

His eyes met mine then, a stormy sea meeting the shore with both trepidation and yearning. "You speak of destiny as though it is within our grasp," he murmured, a vulnerability creeping into his tone that I had not heard before.

"We shape our destiny every day with the choices we make," I replied, feeling the truth of my words deep in my bones. "And today we choose to fight back—to reclaim what has been taken from us."

For a long moment, Eirian remained silent, his internal battle almost palpable in the quiet dawn. Then slowly, as though shedding a layer of doubt that had long encased his heart, he nodded.

"You are right," he conceded with a hesitant yet resolute breath. "We must try."

The forest seemed to exhale with us, a frozen breeze whispering through the trees in subtle approval. We stood there together in shared resolve, two souls bound by a common purpose and an unspoken understanding that whatever lay ahead, we would face it side by side.

I could see the weight of centuries in Eirian's eyes, the burden of a curse that had not only ensnared his form but also his spirit. He stood before me, a being of power and majesty, reduced to a vessel of doubt and fear. It was not just his own pain I saw in those deep, fathomless pools, but the pain of every soul that had ever felt alone, trapped by their own demons.

I stepped closer to him, closing the distance until I could feel the heat emanating from his scaled body. The cold morning air nipped at my skin, but it was nothing compared to the chill of despair that I sought to banish from his heart. "Eirian," I began, my voice a gentle yet unwavering whisper, "I know you're afraid. I am too. But we can't let that fear paralyze us."

His gaze was fixed on me, an anchor in the sea of uncertainty. "Beauty," he said, his voice a low rumble, "this path is full of shadows and thorns. What if—"

"No," I interrupted, placing a finger against his lips. The contact sent a jolt through me—a connection that felt as ancient as the stars above us. "We mustn't dwell on 'what ifs.' We have strength—your strength and mine—and together we can overcome anything."

With a courage bolstered by the rising sun that heralded new beginnings, I reached out and took his massive hand in mine. His skin was rough, calloused by battles long past, yet there was tenderness in the way he allowed me to intertwine our fingers.

"We have to believe in ourselves," I said, my heart hammering against my ribcage with the force of my conviction. My gaze held his, unwavering and fierce. "Together."

A tremor ran through Eirian's hand—the first crack in the fortress he had built around himself. Our eyes remained locked, two souls stripped bare in the dawning light.

In that moment, I knew we were embarking on a journey that would test us in ways we could scarcely imagine. But looking into Eirian's eyes—eyes that had seen too much yet still dared to hope—I saw reflected back at me not just my own determination but something more powerful than any curse: the unyielding spirit of hope.

He squeezed my hand back, a silent vow passing between us without need for words. It was a vow to stand against whatever darkness lay ahead and to do so together. As long as our hearts beat with this shared purpose, we would never truly be alone.

And so we stood there amidst the frozen forest, two dragon hearts beating as one—united by a resolve as enduring as the mountains themselves.

The light of dawn had begun to seep through the canopy, casting a gentle glow that seemed to warm the very air around us. As I stood there, my hand clasped in Eirian's, I could feel the subtle shift in the forest's mood. It was as if the frozen boughs of the trees themselves were leaning in closer, eager to witness the birth of an alliance that could alter the fate of our world.

Eirian's eyes searched mine, and I could see the storm clouds of doubt begin to scatter from his gaze. His expression softened, and the lines of worry that had etched themselves across his brow seemed to smooth. In that moment, it wasn't just the Beast standing before me, but Prince Eirian—the man who still held onto a flicker of hope despite the darkness that had consumed his life.

"Maybe she's right," he murmured, almost to himself. "Maybe we can do this together." His voice was low, a whisper meant only for the two of us amidst the stillness of the forest.

His grip on my hand tightened ever so slightly—a small gesture, yet one that spoke volumes. It was a silent acknowledgment of trust and commitment to our shared goal. My heart swelled with a mixture of pride and affection for this complex creature who had endured so much yet was willing to take a leap of faith with me.

I couldn't help but smile at him, my own heart lifting with his agreement. The surge of excitement and determination within me blossomed like a flame being fed by a gentle breeze. I knew our journey would be fraught with peril, but in that moment, all I felt was the promise of adventure and the bond that was forming between us.

As the sun rose higher, chasing away the last remnants of night, I sensed a transformation—not just in Eirian or myself, but in the very air we breathed. The tension that had hung between us like a heavy cloak fell away, replaced by a sense of cautious optimism that fluttered softly like leaves in a delicate dance.

Eirian nodded slowly, each movement deliberate and infused with newfound resolve. "We go together," he declared, his voice stronger now, carrying through the woods with an authority that seemed to resonate with his true nature as prince and dragon protector.

The forest brightened around us as if in agreement, beams of sunlight piercing through to illuminate our path forward—a path uncertain and fraught with unknowns but one we would traverse side by side. With each other's strength to bolster our courage, perhaps we truly could overcome anything set before us.

And so we stood there, not as Beauty and the Beast but as allies united by purpose—a dragon shifter and a cursed dragon shifter prince ready to reclaim our destinies from the shadows that sought to bind us.

The clearing was a tiny oasis, bathed in the morning light that filtered through the towering trees, casting a dappled pattern on the forest floor. Eirian and I moved about with purpose, yet there was an unspoken ease between us—a camaraderie that had silently woven itself into the fabric of our newfound alliance.

As we gathered our supplies, a mix of excitement and anxiety bubbled within me. My hands worked methodically, packing dried meats, bread, and a flask of water from the nearby stream. Eirian unfurled an old map across a fallen log, his finger tracing the route we'd take. Beside it lay a pair of sturdy swords, their blades gleaming with a promise of protection.

"We should avoid the Marshes of Malador," Eirian's deep voice broke the comfortable silence. "The creatures there are not fond of visitors."

I nodded, glancing at the ominous area he pointed out. "What about the Valley of Whispers?" I asked. "Could it be a safer path?"

"Possibly," he conceded with a thoughtful frown. "But we must be wary of the Echo Bats. Their cries can disorient even the most seasoned traveler."

I tucked away his warnings in my mind as I turned my attention to the amulet that hung heavily around my neck—the source of my newfound abilities. Closing my eyes, I focused on the energy pulsing within it. With a deep breath, I called forth a small flame in my palm. It danced like a living thing, responding to my silent command to grow brighter and then dim.

Eirian watched, his usual guarded expression giving way to one of admiration. "You're learning quickly," he said, an undercurrent of pride in his voice.

The corners of my mouth lifted in response. His approval meant more than I cared to admit. "We're ready," I whispered to myself as much as to him. "This is the start of something extraordinary."

He nodded in agreement, and together we double-checked our packs, ensuring we had everything we might need for the uncertain road ahead. The sunlight seemed to grow warmer around us as if blessing our preparations.

I felt it then—the stirring of something grand and terrifying within me—a dragon's spirit awakening to its full potential. My gaze met Eirian's once more, and I saw my own mixture of hope and trepidation mirrored back at me.

"We'll face whatever comes," he said firmly.

"Yes," I agreed, feeling that same firmness settle in my own chest. "Together."

The path stretched before us, a ribbon of light winding through the frigid forest. It was ominous with the unknown that lay beyond each turn. My heart raced with excitement and determination as Eirian and I stepped onto the trail, our journey finally beginning.

The weight of the Dragon's Heart against my chest was a constant reminder of my purpose and the heritage I was still coming to terms with. I was eager to unravel the mysteries of my bloodline and even more so to help Eirian break free from his curse. Every step we took was a step towards our intertwined destinies.

We walked side by side in comfortable silence, occasionally sharing stories of our pasts. Eirian spoke of his childhood in the castle, of days filled with laughter and nights under starlit skies before darkness had crept into his life. I listened, hanging onto every word, feeling our bond strengthen with each shared memory.

"I remember my mother teaching me about the stars," he said, his voice tinged with a wistfulness that tugged at my heartstrings. "She would say they were our ancestors watching over us."

I smiled at him, warmed by the notion. "Perhaps they're watching over us now," I replied, hoping to offer him some comfort.

Eirian's gaze met mine, and in his eyes, I saw a glimmer of something that might have been gratitude—or maybe it was hope. Our shared journey was fostering trust and companionship between us, something I would have never imagined when I first encountered the fearsome Beast he could become.

Using my newfound abilities felt like tapping into an ancient well of power that had always been inside me. As we navigated through thickets and over streams, I called upon small flames to light our way or willed the earth to steady beneath our feet. Each successful use of my powers bolstered my confidence.

"Every step brings us closer to our goal. We can do this," I whispered under my breath, both as a mantra for myself and a vow for Eirian.

He must have heard me because he nodded once, resolutely. "We will," he affirmed.

Our path wove deeper into the forest, where shafts of icy light pierced through the canopy, casting an ethereal glow on everything they touched. The beauty of it all filled me with awe—this world was so much bigger than the small village I had known all my life.

As we walked on, Eirian began to open up more about his feelings and fears. His honesty made me feel closer to him than ever before; it was as if we were not just allies but friends who had shared a lifetime's worth of experiences in these few precious moments together.

The forest path ahead might have been both inviting and ominous, but with Eirian by my side and the Dragon's Heart around my neck, I felt ready to face whatever lay ahead.

The roar of the river grew deafening as we neared the edge of the treacherous waterway. Frothy waves crashed against jagged rocks, sending a fine mist into the air that clung to my skin like a nervous sweat. Eirian stood beside me, his gaze fixed on the turbulent waters that cut across our path like a living barrier.

"This river wasn't here before," he muttered, his brow furrowing in consternation. "Freya's curse has reshaped the land itself."

Anxiety fluttered in my chest like a caged bird, its wings beating against my ribs. I had never faced such a force of nature before, and doubt whispered in my ear, questioning my abilities as a dragon shifter. But alongside that uncertainty, determination kindled within me, a flame that refused to be snuffed out by fear.

Eirian caught the flicker of apprehension in my eyes and placed a reassuring hand on my shoulder. "We'll find a way across," he said with conviction.

I nodded, squaring my shoulders as I turned to face the raging river. "This is just the beginning," I reminded myself aloud. "We have to trust in our abilities and each other."

Closing my eyes, I reached deep within myself, seeking the connection to the Dragon's Heart that pulsed around my neck. I envisioned a bridge—sturdy and strong—spanning the wild torrent before us. The amulet grew warm against my skin, its glow intensifying as I willed my vision into reality.

With a deep breath, I stretched out my hands toward the river, and from the tips of my fingers, streams of ice began to weave together over the water, intertwining with tendrils of fire that hardened the frost into solid form. A bridge of ice and flame arched gracefully across the river, a testament to the power I was only beginning to understand.

Eirian watched in awe before springing into action. His strength was undeniable as he secured ropes around nearby trees, anchoring our makeshift bridge against the force of the current. Together, we worked with silent efficiency, united by a common goal.

As we finished securing our passage, Eirian turned to me with a look of admiration I had not seen before. "You truly are remarkable," he said earnestly.

I felt a surge of pride at his words—a balm for my lingering self-doubt—and allowed myself a small smile. "Let's see if it holds," I replied with cautious optimism.

We stepped onto the bridge together, Eirian's hand finding mine as we took those first tentative steps over the churning waters below. The bridge held firm beneath our weight, and with each step forward, our confidence grew.

This was just one obstacle on our journey—a journey that promised many more challenges ahead—but as we reached the opposite shore, I knew that together we were capable of facing them all.

The Trial of Fire

Prince Eirian, the Dragon Beast

We had been trekking for days through the frozen tundra, our boots crunching over crystalline drifts. Icy winds whipped at our cloaks, stinging exposed skin. But our fervor pushed us onward, undaunted by winter's harsh embrace.

Then, cresting a ridge, the landscape transformed before our eyes. A vast, smoldering caldera opened up, as if the world itself had been clawed open by terrible talons. Jagged obsidian spires jutted towards the roiling amber sky, backlit by the furious glow of bubbling lava rivers.

Where moments before we had trekked across an endless expanse of frozen tundra, now a smoldering chasm opened up, as if the world had been violently torn asunder. Jagged obsidian spires jutted skyward, their tips glowing dull red from the blazing rivers of lava that oozed and bubbled far below.

The air itself was an assault on my senses. Thick plumes of sulfurous smoke stung my eyes and coated my throat with every rasping breath. The reek of brimstone and charred rock was overwhelming. Yet beneath it all, I could taste the thrumming of primal magic - ancient, untamed, and infinitely more hazardous than the molten hellscape surrounding us.

The ground shuddered and moaned, as if the caldera itself drew breath, reminding all who dared trespass that this was no mere inanimate chasm. It lived and raged, filled with the fury of the world's unshakable core.

I could feel the elemental forces vying for dominance within me, my scales heating as my draconic nature responded to the primordial tumult unfolding before us. Part of me wanted to turn and flee from this cauldron of scathing destruction.

"This place is a crucible," I murmured to myself, my voice barely audible over the roar of the flames and the hiss of molten rock. "It will test us to our limits."

I could feel Beauty's gaze on me, her eyes reflecting the fiery landscape. There was fear there, yes, but overshadowed by an unwavering resolve that stirred something within me. She had come so far, braved so much. I would not let this fiery hell be her end.

I stepped closer to her, drawn by an instinct to protect that I hadn't felt in ages. My dragon's heart knew only isolation and battle, yet here I was, ready to shield another with my very being. It was unsettling—this shift within me—but I couldn't ignore it.

We paused at the edge of the inferno, taking in the treacherous path ahead. The heat was oppressive, wrapping around us like a second skin. I watched as a bead of sweat traced a path down Beauty's cheek before evaporating in an instant.

"Are you ready?" I asked, though it was more for my own sake than hers.

She nodded, her determination steeling my own nerves. "Let's do this."

The terrain was unforgiving; every step required caution as we navigated between jets of flame and unstable ground that threatened to collapse beneath our weight at any moment. My senses were heightened to their utmost limit—each sound and vibration telegraphing potential danger.

As we moved forward, I couldn't help but marvel at Beauty's resilience. Her steps were measured and confident despite the chaos around us. It wasn't just her newfound dragon shifter abilities that impressed me; it was her indomitable spirit.

A sudden explosion of heat and noise had us leaping back as a geyser of lava erupted nearby. We exchanged a glance that conveyed more than words ever could—a mutual acknowledgment of the peril we faced and the trust we placed in each other.

This trial by fire would either forge us into something stronger or consume us entirely. And yet, as I looked at Beauty's profile against the backdrop of dancing flames and molten earth, I realized there was no one else I would rather have by my side.

We pressed on, each step taking us deeper into the heart of the inferno.

Before us stretched a treacherous sea of molten rock, the air shimmering with heat that threatened to sear the very breath from my lungs. A path of jagged stones rose from the fiery waves, a precarious bridge across this hellish expanse. I could feel the intense heat licking at my scales, a stark reminder of the peril we faced.

"I have to ensure every step is safe for her," I thought as I glanced back at Beauty. Her face was set in grim determination, her eyes reflecting the flickering flames that surrounded us. "One misstep could be fatal."

With a deep breath that scorched my throat, I stepped forward onto the first stone, feeling it shift under my weight. My heart pounded, not with fear for myself, but for her. Every muscle in my body tensed as I tested the rock's stability before motioning for Beauty to follow.

We moved in silence, save for the occasional sound of shifting stone or a hiss of steam as it escaped some unseen fissure. Sweat streamed down my face, evaporating before it had a chance to cool my skin.

I dared another glance back at Beauty and saw her pause to steady herself against a tremor that ran through the ground. Our eyes met, and I nodded to reassure her, though I knew she needed no such thing. Her courage was as unwavering as the stones beneath our feet.

The further we ventured into this trial by fire, the more I marveled at her resilience. She was truly her ancestors' heir—fearless and resolute in the face of danger.

As we reached what seemed to be the midpoint of our fiery traverse, I paused to assess the path ahead. The stones grew sparser and smaller; each one would require precise balance and timing.

The earth beneath us convulsed violently, a guttural roar that heralded chaos. I watched, heart hammering against my ribs, as a towering rock formation that had promised safe passage crumbled before our eyes, tumbling into the fiery abyss below. The gap it left was a chasm too vast to cross by any ordinary means, and panic clawed at my throat with its icy fingers.

Beside me, Beauty's breath hitched in a sharp intake. For a fleeting moment, her eyes mirrored the terror that gripped my own soul. But as I turned to her, seeking some sliver of hope in her gaze, I witnessed the transformation that defied the despair.

With a sudden flare of determination igniting in her depths, she raised her hands. Her skin began to shimmer with an ethereal light, the air around us crackling with the power of her dragon lineage. I felt it then—a surge of awe that eclipsed my fear—as ice crystallized from her fingertips, weaving across the molten river in a delicate arc of frost.

She's stronger than she realizes. We can do this if we trust in her abilities.

I barely recognized my own voice as it echoed in my head, a mantra to steady my nerves. She was indeed the last of her kind, a shifter born from legends thought long dead.

The bridge of ice solidified before us, gleaming like a ribbon of moonlight against the nightmarish glow of the lava. Beauty looked at her creation with wide eyes, surprise etching itself into every line of her face. It was clear she had not known the extent of her power until this very moment.

As if pulled by an invisible thread, I reached out and grasped her hand firmly in mine. Our fingers entwined naturally, as though they were meant to fit together this way all along. We stepped onto the bridge together—her hand in mine—our footsteps cautious but unyielding.

Each step on the ice was a testament to Beauty's newfound strength and my burgeoning trust in her. The heat from below seared through our boots, threatening to melt our only path to salvation. Yet, under Beauty's command, the ice held firm—a bulwark against the firestorm raging beneath us.

As we crossed the bridge side by side, I felt something shift within me—a newfound respect for this woman who wielded ice as easily as others might wield a sword. Her powers complemented my own brute force; together we were more than just two cursed souls navigating an unforgiving world.

We were partners in this quest—bound by fate and fire—and I could not help but wonder at what other marvels lay dormant within her, waiting for their chance to awaken and change everything we thought we knew about our journey ahead.

As we neared the edge of the infernal expanse, the ground began to tremble with a deep, menacing rhythm. From the roiling depths of the lava, fire beasts erupted, their bodies aglow with molten fury. They barred our path, their snarls reverberating through the scorching air.

My heart pounded with a surge of protectiveness and an iron-clad determination to fight. Beside me, I felt Beauty tense, her fear palpable yet swiftly replaced by a steely resolve that mirrored my own. I knew then that we had to stand together against this new threat.

Without hesitation, I let my human facade fall away, my body contorting and expanding into the monstrous form that was both my curse and my strength. Scales as dark as obsidian armored my skin, and powerful wings unfurled from my back, casting ominous shadows on the cracked earth. As a dragon beast, I roared a challenge to the fire creatures that dared to confront us.

The fire beasts lunged with a ferocity born of flame itself. My movements were fluid and precise, each strike driven by an instinctive need to protect Beauty. Claws met fiery hide as I battled the creatures, their heat searing even through my scaled protection.

I stole glances at Beauty amidst the fray. She moved with a grace and confidence that captivated me, her hands weaving intricate patterns in the air. Ice blossomed at her command, forming barriers that shielded us from fiery assaults and creating distractions that allowed me to land critical blows upon our enemies. Each graceful movement was a testament to her newfound strength, and the icy constructs she summoned were as formidable as they were beautiful.

Her bravery astounded me; it was as if she had been born for this—to fight alongside a beast of legend against forces that sought to kill us. She faced the fire creatures with a fierce determination, her eyes blazing with an inner fire that matched their own. In that moment, I realized that Beauty was not just an ally or a companion; she was a warrior, every bit as powerful and essential to our survival as I was.

Her ice clashed against their flames, sizzling in the heated air as it quenched their ardor. With each beast that fell before us, our synergy grew stronger—two halves of a whole united against a common foe.

I realized then that this journey was not just about breaking curses or discovering destinies; it was about finding trust in one another—in her strength as much as in mine. Together we stood resolute amidst the chaos, our combined might an unbreakable force against all that threatened to tear us apart.

The last ember of the fire beasts flickered out, and the world fell silent save for the distant murmur of the lava. We stood there, Beauty and I, breathing heavily, our bodies battered from the fight. Relief washed over me like a gentle wave, leaving behind a sense of accomplishment that was foreign yet intoxicating. But as the adrenaline waned, so too did my strength, revealing the extent of our injuries.

We needed respite—a moment to gather ourselves before pressing on. With weary steps, we sought refuge on a patch of ground that was mercifully free from the scorching heat. As we settled down, I felt the tremor of my muscles and the sting of my wounds—a stark reminder of our vulnerability.

Beauty's gaze met mine, a silent understanding passing between us. Without a word, she extended her hands, palms facing upward. The air around us cooled as she summoned her powers once more, this time weaving a delicate mist that seemed to dance with life. It spiraled upward, enveloping us in its soothing embrace.

I watched in quiet awe as the mist kissed my skin, its cool touch bringing relief to the burns and cuts that marred my flesh. "She's remarkable," I thought, my heart swelling with an emotion I couldn't quite name. We were indeed stronger together—her ice and my fire intertwined in a symphony of survival.

As I bandaged a wound on my arm, wincing at the pull of torn skin, I kept my eyes on Beauty. She worked with careful precision, tending to her own injuries with an elegance that belied her fatigue. The mist she had conjured clung to her like a cloak made of morning dew, highlighting the strength that lay beneath her gentle exterior.

Gratitude welled up within me—a gratitude not just for the healing but for her presence by my side. It was an unfamiliar feeling for someone who had long embraced solitude as an uninvited companion. Yet here she was: Beauty, who had walked into my cursed life and transformed it in ways I had not dared to dream.

Our conversation was sparse; words seemed inadequate against the magnitude of what we had endured together. But in those moments of shared silence, our bond deepened—a bond forged in fire and solidified in ice.

I caught myself studying her profile as she rested against a boulder, her chest rising and falling with each breath. The trials ahead loomed large in my mind—uncertain and fraught with danger—but so too did my resolve to face them with her by my side.

As Beauty's gentle breathing filled the silence of our makeshift sanctuary, a turmoil churned within me, its claws sharper than those that tipped my fingers. I lay there, feigning rest, my gaze lingering on her peaceful face. How could she lie so serene when inside me raged a storm of doubts and fears?

She stirred slightly, and instinctively, my muscles tensed, ready to leap to her defense should some unseen threat approach. But the only danger here was the one that resided within my own skin—the beast that I had become. It was a constant battle to keep the monster at bay, to present a facade of strength and confidence when, in truth, I was nothing but a mass of insecurities.

"I can't let her see my doubts," I thought fiercely. "She needs to believe in me, even if I can't believe in myself." This mantra became a shield against the vulnerability threatening to spill from the cracks in my armored heart.

I forced a smile as she woke, though it felt as if it were carved from stone. My jaw tightened with the effort of maintaining this masquerade. I could not allow her to glimpse the darkness that gnawed at my soul—the fear that she might one day look upon me and see only the monster, not the man.

Gratitude for her presence warred with the dread of disappointing her. She deserved someone whole, someone unmarred by curses and rage. Yet here she was with me—someone who had more in common with nightmares than with heroes.

As Beauty sat up and stretched, oblivious to my internal struggle, she offered me a smile that held the warmth of dawn after a night of shadows. It was a smile that reached deep into the recesses of my being, stirring something long buried beneath layers of self-loathing and regret.

How could she not see the sharp edges of my nature? How could she not feel the danger that lurked beneath my skin? And yet she treated me with kindness and an unwavering trust that left me both humbled and terrified.

She spoke then, her voice soft but filled with an underlying strength that had come to define her. "We should get moving soon," she said.

I nodded in agreement, rising to gather our belongings while hiding the tremble in my hands. I was adept at wearing armor—both literal and figurative—but Beauty's presence made it increasingly difficult to keep it fastened tight.

As we prepared to continue our journey, I steeled myself for what lay ahead. I would protect her; I would fight for her; I would be the shield against all threats. For Beauty's sake—and perhaps even for my own—I would not falter.

But deep down, where fears ran as deep as ancient caverns, I knew this path would test me in ways I could scarcely imagine. Would I be strong enough? Could I truly be more than the beast? Only time would tell...

The dawn greeted us with a sky painted in hues of frozen color, a stark contrast to the smoldering landscape we had traversed the day before. The fire beasts and their infernal domain lay behind us, and as I watched the sun ascend, I felt the icy grip of dread that had held my heart begin to thaw. Today was a new day, and with Beauty by my side, it seemed even fate itself might bow to our will.

We worked in silent harmony, gathering our sparse belongings and dousing the remnants of our campfire. Each movement was methodical, conserving energy for the unknown path ahead. As I rolled up the makeshift map we had been charting, Beauty's hand brushed against mine, a simple touch that sent a jolt of warmth through my veins.

"We've faced the fire together," I found myself murmuring. The words felt like an incantation, a vow that solidified the bond between us. Whatever came next, we would face it as a team.

Beauty glanced up at me, her eyes reflecting the light of the rising sun. "And we'll face whatever comes next together too," she affirmed, her voice steady with conviction.

I nodded, feeling an unfamiliar surge of optimism. It was cautious yet genuine—a sense that perhaps we were not so ill-fated after all. With each passing moment, Beauty's powers grew more impressive, more radiant. She was becoming not just an ally but a beacon of hope in my shadowed existence.

Her grip on my hand was firm as we set off. I matched her stride with newfound confidence; the challenges ahead no longer seemed insurmountable with her by my side. Our footsteps were in sync, leaving a trail of unity across the soft earth.

The searing heat and noxious fumes of the volcanic caldera gradually fell away with each step. What had started as smoldering, cracked badlands slowly transmuted into an icy desolation that chilled me to my core.

The ground, once radiating waves of volcanic energy, now crunched beneath my talons with every stride across the thickening permafrost. Beauty shuddered and pulled her cloak tighter as frigid gusts whipped around us, leaching away what little warmth remained.

The very air seemed to crystallize with each rattling exhale, plumes of vapor swirling in the eddying currents sweeping down from the looming, snow-capped peaks. Where once choking veils of sulfurous smoke had stung our eyes and throats, now an eerie, oppressive silence descended, muffling the world under an suffocating blanket of white.

Beauty's voice broke through the oppressive silence, rich with that fiery determination that had sustained us through so many chilling ordeals.

"We have quite the journey ahead," she said, pulling her cloak tighter against the biting gusts.

I rumbled an acknowledgment, stamping my talons against the frozen tundra in an attempt to revive their fading warmth. The icy wastelands stretched endlessly in every direction, an unbroken expanse of desolate white. Just looking out across that frigid infinitude seeped the vigor from my limbs.

But Beauty was unswayed. Pivoting to face me, I saw that familiar blazing glint kindling in the depths of her eyes. It was a defiant spark, one that refused to be snuffed out no matter how fiercely the Arctic gales tried to extinguish it.

"I won't let this frozen waste chill my spirit," she declared, the words carrying the heat of inner furnaces. "We've endured the torment of fire and ash. What's a little ice to those who have conquered the scorching path?"

"Yes," I agreed. "But we have already overcome much."

She smiled then—a smile that reached deep into my chest and coiled around my heart like ivy. "Together," she reminded me.

Together indeed. It was a word that held power—a promise of shared burdens and shared victories. It was not just an acknowledgment of our partnership but an embrace of what we could become.

As we walked hand in hand towards whatever destiny awaited us, I allowed myself to believe in that future—a future where curses could be broken and love could prevail. A future where even a beast might find redemption in the eyes of beauty.

Rival Encounters

Beauty

The frozen wasteland stretched out before us, a desolate expanse where the sun's weak rays barely penetrated the perpetual twilight. The ground was a mix of ice and snow, each step crunching beneath our feet as we trudged through the bleak terrain. I breathed in sharply, the air so cold it felt like shards of glass in my lungs, as Eirian and I navigated the endless white expanse and jagged ice formations. My heart held a mix of awe at the stark, icy beauty around us and a thread of caution; this land was ancient and unforgiving, and I could feel the remnants of powerful magic buried deep beneath the frost.

I kept close to Eirian, his towering form a reassuring presence in this vast, unchanging landscape. His steps were steady and confident, even in the biting cold, and I found myself matching my pace to his. The eerie silence of the wasteland was occasionally broken by the distant howl of the wind, and despite the apparent desolation, I felt eyes upon us, the ghosts of long-forgotten beings watching from the shadows of the ice.

Our breath formed misty clouds in the frigid air, and every exhale seemed to crystallize before falling to the ground. The frozen wilderness lulled me into a false sense of security with its deceptive stillness, but the lessons of recent days kept my eyes darting from ice mound to ice mound, wary of hidden dangers lurking beneath the snow.

As we pressed on, a faint sound reached my ears—a crunch of snow that did not come from our own steps. My heart quickened, and I strained to listen over the howling wind. There it was again, closer this time. I glanced at Eirian, who had also heard it, his eyes narrowing as he scanned the horizon.

Then, I saw them—dark figures moving silently through the snow, their forms barely discernible against the white backdrop. They lurked ominously at the edge of our vision, their presence sending a chill down my spine that had nothing to do with the cold. I gripped Eirian's arm, my voice a tense whisper. "We're not alone."

Eirian nodded, his gaze fixed on the figures. "Stay close," he said, his voice low and calm, but I could sense the tension in his stance. We continued forward, every sense heightened, as the figures followed us, a silent threat in the frozen wasteland.

"Who are they? What do they want from us?" The thought fluttered in my mind like a trapped bird as we ventured deeper into the forest's heart.

A rustle to our right had me halting in my tracks. Eirian's hand shot out, pulling me behind him as figures emerged from the shadows. Their eyes glinted with malice and something darker, a hunger for power that sent shivers down my spine. They circled us like predators, their movements eerily synchronized.

My pulse quickened as I took a step back, my hand instinctively reaching for the amulet around my neck. It pulsed with a warmth that seeped into my palm, steadying my nerves. Their leader, I learned his name was Draven fixed his gaze on me, sharp and assessing, and I felt the weight of his ambition pressing against my chest.

Eirian's growl rumbled low in his throat, a warning that vibrated through the air. "What do you want?" he demanded, his voice a mix of command and challenge.

Draven's lips curled into a smirk. "The last heir of the dragon shifters," he said, his eyes never leaving my amulet. "You're coming with us."

I felt Eirian's protective presence like a shield at my back. "Over my dead body," he retorted.

A surge of fear gripped me, but it was quickly replaced by an unwavering determination. These rivals would not deter us from our quest; they would not take me without a fight. My fingers curled into fists as I prepared to stand beside Eirian, to defend what we had started together.

"Let them try," I whispered under my breath, feeling the dragon fire within me stir to life.

Draven's laugh was a hollow sound that bounced eerily off the trees. "You are a means to an end—the key to power beyond measure." His eyes flicked toward the amulet that lay against my chest, its glow muted but steadfast.

"We can't back down now," I thought fiercely. "We have to show them we mean no harm." But as Draven stepped closer, I knew our chances of a peaceful resolution were slipping away like sand through fingers.

Eirian moved slightly in front of me, a silent sentinel. His body was tense, ready to spring into action at any moment. I could feel the heat radiating from him—a reminder of the beast within.

Draven's followers fanned out, their hands resting on the hilts of their swords, their postures mirroring their leader's aggression. "The Ice Queen will be pleased to have you," Draven continued, his words slicing through the fragile peace of the forest.

I felt Eirian's hand brush mine, a silent message of unity and strength. My heart pounded in my chest, but his touch steadied me. Together, we were more than just two cursed souls—we were a force to be reckoned with.

"You will not take her," Eirian growled, his voice low and dangerous.

Draven tilted his head, considering us with a predator's patience. "Then we shall see if fire or ice will claim victory today."

As he signaled his followers to advance, I knew there was no turning back. Every fiber of my being screamed for me to fight, to defend our right to seek freedom from our burdens. The bond between

Eirian and me had been forged in trials by fire and ice—it would not be broken by those who coveted power over compassion.

I squared my shoulders and prepared to face whatever came next, with Eirian at my side and the courage of my ancestors blazing within me.

The forest erupted into chaos, its once tranquil expanse transforming into a battlefield charged with raw energy. Flashes of dragon magic lit up the trees as Eirian and I moved in unison, our attacks a symphony of flame and shadow against Draven's encroaching forces.

Adrenaline surged through my veins, fear sharp and clear, but beneath it all burned a fierce determination. We were fighting for more than just our survival—we were fighting for the very soul of Eirian and Eldoria. The thought was a beacon in the tumult, grounding me even as swords clashed and powers roared around us.

"We can do this," I thought as I ducked a swinging blade, "Together, we're stronger." It was a mantra that pulsed with every beat of my heart, lending strength to my limbs.

With each carefully coordinated move, Eirian and I demonstrated a growing trust—a dance of combat learned through trials by fire and ice. My newfound abilities as a dragon shifter became more pronounced with every breath I took. Scales shimmered across my skin in flashes of iridescent light, and when I breathed out, the air crackled with energy.

I glanced at Eirian, his own power unfurling in magnificent displays of might. He fought fiercely by my side, his presence both comforting and empowering. Each time our eyes met amidst the fray, there was an unspoken vow exchanged—a promise to protect each other until the end.

Draven's followers were relentless, but they had underestimated the bond between two dragon hearts. As we fought back-to-back, our combined might began to turn the tide. Draven's eyes narrowed as he witnessed the true extent of our powers.

With every blow I landed, my confidence swelled. These rivals sought to claim the Dragon's Heart for themselves, but they would find no victory here. Not against the last heir of the dragon shifters and her valiant protector.

Eirian let out a roar that shook the leaves from their branches, and I felt that roar within me too—a call to rise above fear and claim the strength that was my birthright. The ice-covered forest may have become our battleground today, but it would also bear witness to our unwavering resolve.

As Draven's forces closed in, a hush fell over the forest. A figure emerged, her presence like a calm eye in the storm of our battle. Selene stood there, a neutral dragon shifter with an aura of undeniable authority. "Enough!" she commanded, and even Draven's warriors hesitated, their swords lowering just enough to signal a pause.

I caught my breath, feeling the sweat and soot on my brow. Selene's gaze met mine, and in that moment, I understood she held a different kind of power—one that could sway the tide of this confrontation without a single drop of blood.

"We can end this madness," Selene said, her voice resonating with a strength that belied her calm demeanor. "You seek to break Freya's curse, and they," she gestured to Draven and his followers, "wish only to live free from her tyranny. An alliance could benefit us all."

Caution flickered in my eyes as I weighed her words. My heart yearned for any advantage we could grasp, yet the fear of betrayal was a bitter pill. *This could be the chance we need,* I thought warily. *But can we trust them?*

Draven stepped forward, his expression unreadable. "We want no part in Freya's games. We only want to live free again," he admitted grudgingly. "Our fight is not with you."

Eirian stood silent beside me, his body coiled like a spring. I turned to him, our eyes locking in silent conversation. His nod was cautious but certain—trust was a risk we had to take.

"We accept," I said finally, my voice steady despite the tumultuous emotions within me. "But know this: any sign of treachery, and our alliance ends."

Selene nodded, satisfied. "Then let us discuss terms." She looked at each of us in turn, ensuring our commitment.

I felt hope fluttering in my chest, tempered by the weight of apprehension. The decision to ally with Draven's faction was not made lightly; it was a strategic move that could either save us or doom us all.

As we outlined our cooperation, the icy realm seemed to hold its breath along with us. Every word spoken was a step toward an uncertain future—one that I hoped would lead us out of darkness and into light.

Eirian's hand found mine once more, his touch grounding me as we forged this fragile new bond with those who were once our enemies. There was strength in unity, and though the path ahead was fraught with danger, I knew we would face it together.

The air of tension began to dissipate as an uneasy peace settled over us all—a peace that would be tested in the days to come but held the promise of freedom from Freya's icy grasp.

The campfire crackled softly, its warm glow bathing our faces in a gentle light that seemed to soften the harshness of the world around us. The icy landscape around us receded into the backdrop, a silent witness to the quiet intimacy of the moment. I reached for a cloth, dampened it with water from our supplies, and turned my attention to Eirian.

He sat shirtless, his broad shoulders marred by the battle's toll, yet he exuded a stoic endurance that only deepened my respect for him. I could see the way his muscles tensed in anticipation of pain as I approached, but he didn't flinch when I began to clean his wounds.

"Eirian," I whispered, my voice barely rising above the crackling of the flames. "This might sting."

He merely nodded, his eyes fixed on mine with an intensity that held a world of unspoken words. As I tended to him, my touch gentle but sure, I felt a profound tenderness well up within me. His vulnerability in this moment—allowing me to care for him—touched something deep in my heart.

He's been through so much, I thought as I moved to a particularly nasty cut on his arm. *I want to help him heal, in every way.* Not just the physical scars, but the emotional ones that lingered beneath his rugged exterior.

My hands were steady as they worked, though my heart raced with an emotion that was new and frightening in its intensity. It was more than just compassion or the bond formed from shared trials; it was a protective instinct laced with affection that went beyond our mission or the roles we had assumed.

As I dabbed at a gash on his chest, Eirian winced slightly but quickly masked it with a wry smile. "I've had worse," he said, though there was a softness in his eyes that belied his casual tone.

"I know," I replied, meeting his gaze. "But you don't have to endure it alone anymore."

The silence that followed was filled with understanding and something more—a connection that seemed to grow stronger with each shared glance and touch. We talked then, our conversation meandering from fears and uncertainties to hopes for what lay ahead.

His guarded expression softened as we spoke, revealing a trust in me that made my chest swell with emotion. In turn, I found myself opening up to him about my own doubts and dreams—a vulnerability I had never allowed myself to show anyone before.

In this quiet space by the firelight, where shadows danced and time seemed to stand still, Eirian and I found solace in each other's presence. Our journey was uncertain and fraught with danger, but here and now, we were simply two souls seeking comfort in the warmth of shared humanity.

Dawn's pale light filtered through the jagged ice formations, casting shimmering patterns on the frozen ground as I wandered away from our makeshift camp. My thoughts were a tangled web of anticipation and unease, each step crunching through the snow and taking me further into the unknown. That's when I saw it—an ancient stone tablet, half-buried in ice and frost, as if waiting for centuries just for me.

The stone tablet was weathered, its ancient inscriptions faint but legible. My fingers traced the symbols, each one pulsing with a strange familiarity that quickened my heartbeat. Excitement and awe filled me as the inscriptions revealed secrets of my lineage. The knowledge felt like a missing piece of my identity, long lost and now returned.

"This is incredible," I murmured to myself. "It explains so much about who I am and what I can do." The runes spoke of the dragon shifters' heritage, of their might and their bond with the very essence of Eldoria. It wasn't just history; it was a guide to the powers that coursed through my veins—powers I was only beginning to understand.

I studied the tablet intently, every word etching itself into my memory. The true extent of my abilities unfolded before me, vast and thrilling. It was as if I had been given a key to unlock doors I hadn't even known existed within myself.

I needed to share this discovery with Eirian and our new allies. With a surge of confidence and purpose, I hurried back to camp, clutching the knowledge like a precious gem. As I approached, Eirian looked up from tending to the fire, his piercing gaze meeting mine.

"We have hope," I said, barely containing my excitement. "The tablet—it holds answers about my lineage and powers."

Eirian rose to his feet, crossing the distance between us in a few strides. "Show me," he said with an intensity that matched my own.

Together we pored over the inscriptions by the firelight, his presence a solid reassurance by my side. As we deciphered each line, his expression shifted from curiosity to admiration.

"A true heir of dragon shifters," he said softly, his eyes not leaving mine. "I knew you were special, Beauty."

His words sent warmth flooding through me, more invigorating than any flame. With Eirian's pride and support bolstering me, I felt an unshakeable resolve settle in my chest.

We had found something invaluable today—not just knowledge of my heritage but a deeper understanding between us. And with that understanding came a shared determination to face whatever lay ahead on our journey to break Freya's curse.

As I gathered my belongings, the leather of my pack creaked in protest, mirroring the resistance that had once weighed heavy in my heart. But now, there was a sense of purpose in my movements, a clarity that came from understanding my heritage. The icy wasteland around us was eerily silent, the stillness broken only by the occasional whisper of the wind and the promise of new beginnings. Eirian stood beside me, his presence a constant source of strength. We had both been through trials that seemed insurmountable, yet here we were, preparing to face what lay ahead together. "We've come so far," I murmured, not just to him but to myself as well. My fingers brushed against the amulet around my neck, its pulse in sync with my own. "And there's still a long way to go. But I know we can do this together."

He nodded, his eyes reflecting the same determination that coursed through me. Our bond had been forged in fire and fear, but it was now tempered by mutual respect and an unspoken vow to see our quest through to its end.

Around us, our allies were a motley crew bound by a common cause. We had found them—or perhaps they had found us—each with their own reasons for joining our fight against Freya's icy grip on

Eldoria. As we strategized our next move, voices rose and fell in earnest discussion, but when Eirian spoke, everyone listened.

"We head east at dawn," he declared, his voice carrying the weight of his royal lineage. "Freya's castle is said to be guarded by creatures of legend. We must be prepared for anything."

The group murmured their assent, and as they dispersed to ready themselves for departure, Eirian turned to me. His hand found mine, and for a moment we stood in silence, letting the gravity of our shared mission settle over us.

I looked up at him and saw not just the prince or the beast he believed himself to be but the man who had walked through shadows to stand by my side. "Eirian," I said softly, "we will break this curse. Not just for Eldoria but for you."

His grip on my hand tightened briefly before he released it, stepping back with a nod of acknowledgment. As we each returned to our tasks, I felt a surge of something more than hope—it was belief.

The icy wasteland had indeed become a place of renewed hope and purpose—a reminder that even in lands touched by darkness, life found a way to push through. With each knot I tied and each item I stowed away in my pack, anticipation bubbled within me. The frostbitten landscape, with its shimmering ice and snow-covered ground, stood as a testament to resilience and the promise of new beginnings.

I looked at Eirian one more time before shouldering my pack. Together we were ready for whatever came next—united in resolve and strengthened by the truth of who we were: allies bound by destiny and hearts fueled by courage.

Flashbacks and Secrets

Prince Eirian, the Dragon Beast

The morning light barely penetrated the thick blanket of snow that covered the landscape, casting a pale glow over the frozen expanse. The wind howled relentlessly, a constant reminder of the curse that gripped our land in its icy claws. As we trudged through the snow, each step was a battle against the biting cold, but the determination in Beauty's eyes fueled my resolve to press on.

Our journey had brought us to the edge of the frozen mountains, where legends spoke of hidden secrets and ancient knowledge buried deep within. My heart was a tumultuous mix of hope and trepidation, the weight of our quest bearing down heavily upon me. The thought of breaking Freya's curse and restoring peace to our kingdom was a beacon in the darkness, guiding our every move.

The cave loomed before us, a gaping maw in the frozen mountainside, as if the very earth had cracked open to reveal its hidden secrets. Beauty and I exchanged a glance, the weight of our journey pressing upon us like the snow that blanketed the world outside.

As we stepped into the cave, the cold seemed to retreat, replaced by an eerie stillness that enveloped us. The walls were lined with shelves carved into the rock itself, groaning under the weight of countless tomes and scrolls. The air was thick with the scent of old parchment, a testament to knowledge long undisturbed.

I reached out, my fingers grazing the spine of a leather-bound manuscript, its cover cracked and worn. "What truths will these forgotten pages reveal? Can we bear to face them?" I murmured, more to myself than to Beauty. She simply nodded, her eyes alight with a fire that contrasted starkly with the chill of our surroundings.

The dim light filtering through cracks in the cave walls danced upon dust motes that swirled in our wake. Each step we took kicked up a silent storm of forgotten years. My heart pounded with a mix of curiosity and dread as I carefully opened a dusty tome, its pages protesting with a crackle.

We delved deeper into the cave's heart, our hands brushing against ancient amulets and faded maps. One manuscript in particular caught my eye—a treatise on ancient curses and their counters. With trembling hands, I turned its pages, seeking any knowledge that might help us break Freya's curse.

My breath hitched as I stumbled upon a passage detailing a curse strikingly similar to my own affliction—a dragon's form taken as punishment, a beast's visage masking a noble heart. Beside it lay an amulet, its gemstone dark and inscrutable.

Beauty leaned over my shoulder, her presence both comforting and grounding. "Could this be it?" she whispered, her voice tinged with hope.

"I... I'm not sure," I admitted, my throat tight with emotion. The implications of what lay before us were vast—could this truly be the key to unraveling my curse?

As we pored over the ancient texts, time seemed to blur, the outside world fading away until there was only the rustle of pages and our shared breaths in the silence. Every so often, Beauty would reach out to brush away the dust or offer an encouraging smile that bolstered my resolve.

Here in this sacred repository of lost knowledge, we were hunters in search of redemption—seeking answers within ink and parchment that might just set us free.

The cold air of the cave seemed to whisper secrets of a time long past as Beauty and I delved deeper into the ancient texts. Each word, each line we uncovered felt like a step closer to understanding the curse that bound me. The cave's dim light flickered, casting eerie shadows on the walls, amplifying the weight of our discoveries. My fingers traced the delicate script of a particularly weathered manuscript, its leather cover worn from centuries of handling.

As I opened the tome, I felt a strange, almost electric energy course through me. My breath quickened, and I glanced at Beauty, whose eyes reflected the same mix of anticipation and apprehension that churned within me. The words on the page seemed to glow faintly, inviting me to speak them aloud, as if they were meant to be more than silent history.

Taking a deep breath, I began to read, my voice echoing off the cold stone walls of the cave. "And so it was decreed, under the eyes of the starless sky, that the bond between our houses would be severed by blood and betrayal." The words seemed to weave a spell of their own, pulling me into a vision so sharp and real it stole my breath.

The grand hall of our ancestors materialized before me—a place of power and conflict, where voices rose and fell like crashing waves. The air was thick with tension, and the bitter sting of betrayal hung heavy as my forebears argued fiercely. Accusations were hurled with venomous force, and each word seemed to etch itself into my very soul.

A pang of sorrow and guilt twisted in my chest. I witnessed their pride and anger, vices that now shackled me to a monstrous fate. "Our ancestors' mistakes still haunt us," I murmured to myself. "Can we overcome their legacy?"

The scene unfolded with a grim inevitability; the seeds of our families' ruin were sown with every spiteful retort. It was not just a clash of words but of ideals, each one cleaving deeper into bonds once thought unbreakable. And there I stood, invisible among them, a silent witness to the folly that cursed my bloodline.

My fists clenched involuntarily as the weight of inherited guilt bore down upon me. A glance towards Beauty revealed her face, mirroring my own shock and determination. The vision rendered me immobile, a prisoner within my own mind, yet desperate to reach out to her.

In that grand hall, filled with shouting and accusations, I saw the moment when hatred eclipsed kinship—when one vengeful act set forth a cascade of darkness that would span generations. My ancestor's eyes blazed with an all-consuming fury as he cast an irrevocable curse upon her family.

I could feel it—the very moment when our destinies entwined with thorns and shadows. And amidst the clamor and chaos, a single truth resonated within me: this ancient grudge was mine to bear, mine to end.

The ghostly echoes of our ancestors' quarrels faded, leaving us enveloped in the silence of the cave. It was then that Beauty's fingers brushed against a leather-bound journal, its cover worn and edges frayed. With a gentle touch, she opened it, her eyes widening as she deciphered the ancient, faded ink. Each word seemed to lift from the pages, wrapping around her like whispers of a long-forgotten legacy.

I stood beside her, watching as she absorbed the weight of her heritage. The journal belonged to her ancestor, a dragon shifter of formidable power and wisdom. Her fingers traced the lines of text, and I could see the flicker of recognition in her eyes—like she was meeting a part of herself that had always been waiting in the shadows.

Pride swelled within me as I observed her transformation. This unassuming woman from Eldoria was blossoming into something far greater than she had ever imagined. "She's discovering her true strength," I thought. "Together, we can break this curse."

She shared the revelations with a voice that trembled not with fear but with awakening strength. The journal spoke of trials overcome and battles won, of a lineage steeped in magic and courage. It held insights into her unique abilities and hinted at the key to unlocking her full potential—a potential that resonated with every beat of my own cursed heart.

My gaze softened with admiration as I listened. Here before me was not just Beauty but a fierce dragon shifter whose blood sang with ancient power. Involuntarily, my hand reached out to rest upon her shoulder—a gesture meant to comfort but also to acknowledge the bond between us that deepened with every passing moment.

Her eyes met mine, filled with a mixture of determination and newfound confidence that made my heart swell with pride. It was as if the amulet around her neck glowed brighter, reflecting the fire that kindled within her soul.

This journey had started as my search for redemption—a way to reclaim my humanity from beneath the scales and fangs that had become my prison. But now it was our quest, one that bound our fates together more tightly than any spell could weave.

As we turned our attention back to the journal, I knew we were on the cusp of something monumental. The answers we sought were within reach; it was only a matter of time before they would reveal themselves and grant us the power to forge a new destiny—one free from the shadows of our past.

I brushed aside the cobwebs and my hand landed upon an object that sent a chill down my spine. It was a relic of my family's legacy, a dagger with a handle shaped like the snarling maw of a dragon. The metal shimmered with a faint, eerie light, as if echoing the smoldering rage of generations past. Its edge was still sharp, a testament to the deadly intent it once served.

"My family's pride," I whispered, the words catching in my throat. I could feel the weight of history pressing down on me, as heavy as the stone that entombed us in this ancient place. The dagger seemed to beckon me into its dark history, pulling me into a vivid flashback of my family's past.

There they stood, my ancestors, their faces twisted with scorn and arrogance. The scene played out like a macabre dance, their movements fueled by pride and desperation. A heavy sense of responsibility settled over me as I witnessed their desperate actions—the choices that led to this curse that now bound me.

"My family's actions set this tragedy in motion," I realized with a gut-wrenching clarity. "It's up to me to make things right." My fingers curled around the cold hilt of the dagger as if by holding it, I could somehow absorb the sins of my forefathers and forge a new path.

I looked up to find Beauty watching me, her eyes filled with an unwavering support that pierced through the gloom of the cave. It was her strength that had guided us here, her belief in me that had shattered my isolation. My expression hardened with resolve as I met her gaze.

"We will undo what has been done," I promised her—and myself. This relic was more than just a weapon; it was a symbol of the twisted legacy I had inherited. But as I held it now, it felt different. It felt like a key—one that could unlock redemption not just for myself but for our intertwined fates.

The echo of ancient voices began to fade, replaced by the steady drip of water from stalactites overhead. The past would not release its grip easily, but in Beauty's presence, I felt something stir within me—a renewed determination to atone for my ancestors' sins and protect her at all costs.

My grip on the dagger tightened as we prepared to delve deeper into the mysteries and trials that awaited us. With each step forward, we carried not only the hopes of our own hearts but also the chance to mend the fractures left by those who came before us.

The weight of our discoveries hung between us like a tangible shroud as we sat in the shadowy recesses of the cave. Our backs pressed against the cool, damp stone, we found solace in the silence that enveloped us—a respite from the whirlwind of revelations that had swept through our minds.

I felt a tumultuous mix of guilt and hope churning within me, each emotion battling for dominance. The guilt of my family's prideful mistakes weighed heavily on my shoulders, a burden I had borne in the form of scales and claws. Yet, amidst that guilt, a seedling of hope took root—the hope that we could mend what had been shattered so long ago.

"We have to break this cycle," I murmured, more to myself than to Beauty. "Our future depends on it." The words echoed softly in the cavernous space, carrying with them the weight of centuries-old feuds and the fervent desire for a new beginning.

I glanced at Beauty, her face illuminated by the faint light that danced across her features from the amulet around her neck. She looked back at me with an understanding that transcended words, her eyes reflecting not just her own resolve but also a shared conviction that together we could overcome the darkness of our past.

Slowly, I reached out and took her hand in mine. The warmth of her touch spread through me like a balm, soothing the jagged edges of my soul. It was more than just physical comfort—it was the strength I found in her presence, the unwavering support that anchored me when doubts threatened to pull me under.

Her fingers intertwined with mine, a silent vow that neither of us would face what lay ahead alone. In that simple gesture, I felt our connection deepen through shared understanding and purpose. We were two halves of a whole, bound together by destiny and by a love that had begun to bloom amidst adversity.

The cavern's air, thick with the weight of our shared histories, felt charged as we sat there, side by last. Our hands were still clasped, each of us finding an anchor in the other. I looked at Beauty, her face a mere whisper away from mine, lit by the ethereal glow of the Dragon's Heart around her neck. The light seemed to weave an intimate cocoon around us, separating us from the cold, harsh world outside.

A powerful blend of longing and fear coursed through me as I leaned closer. I could feel the warmth of her breath against my skin, each exhale a silent beckoning. My eyes searched hers, delving into the depths of courage and compassion that had drawn me to her from the beginning. She was my unexpected reprieve from a life of solitude and sorrow—a beacon that had pierced through my self-imposed darkness.

"I want to protect her with everything I have. But is it enough?" The thought was a shadow that flitted across my mind, threatening to eclipse the moment. My heart throbbed with a deep ache of desire and connection—a yearning for something more profound than I'd ever allowed myself to feel.

Our faces were so close now that I could count the flecks of gold in her eyes, each one a tiny sun igniting flames within me. Her lips parted slightly, as if she too was contemplating the precipice we found ourselves on—the brink of a chasm filled with the unknown.

The air between us was electric, their eyes locked in an intense gaze as they leaned closer. A powerful blend of longing and fear coursed through me as I leaned closer, our lips almost touching. "I want to protect her with everything I have. But is it enough?" my breath caught, and I feel a deep ache of desire and connection. I pulled back, my eyes reflecting my internal struggle.

But as our lips hovered mere inches apart, reality intruded upon us like a cold draught sneaking through the cracks in ancient stone. I pulled back ever so slightly, my breath catching in my throat. The reflection in Beauty's eyes mirrored my own internal struggle—a longing tempered by the fear of what it would mean to cross that invisible line between us.

In that suspended moment, I realized that this—this closeness—was as perilous as any dragon or curse we might face on our journey. For if I allowed myself this indulgence, if I succumbed to this desire to truly know her in every sense of the word, there would be no turning back.

Her breath mingled with mine in the silence that followed, each exhale a wordless confession of shared vulnerability. And though our lips did not meet in that instant, something unspoken passed between us—an acknowledgment of the bond that was forming, unbreakable and profound.

With a quiet intensity burning in my chest, I pulled back completely, putting space between us once more. We both knew without saying it that there would be time for such explorations later—when we were not standing on such precarious ground.

The tension lingered like morning mist as we turned our gaze forward once again, readying ourselves for whatever lay ahead in the shadowed corridors of our fate.

The musty air of the cave was thick with the residue of revelations long buried, now unearthed by our hands and hearts. As we prepared to leave the sheltering embrace of the ancient stone, I could feel a palpable shift within me—a metamorphosis not of form, but of spirit. The weight of our discoveries bore down upon me, yet it was not a burden; it was an anchor, grounding me in newfound purpose.

Armed with the knowledge that our histories were entwined in a tapestry more complex than either of us could have imagined, we gathered the manuscripts scattered around us. Each page was a piece of the puzzle, a fragment of the past that would guide our steps into an uncertain future. The amulets we collected were not merely trinkets but keys to unlocking powers that lay dormant within us—powers that might turn the tide in the battles to come.

"We're stronger together," I whispered to Beauty as we packed away the last of the scrolls into our weathered satchels. "We'll face whatever comes next." My voice was steady, resolute—a far cry from the ragged whispers that had once echoed through these caverns.

As I stood, I felt taller than I had in years—not in stature but in resolve. My gaze found Beauty's, and in her eyes, I saw not just my reflection but also the reflection of who we could become. She looked back at me with a mix of admiration and determination that mirrored my own. There was no fear there, no hesitation—only an unspoken promise that together we would rise to meet whatever challenges lay ahead.

The artifacts and lore we now possessed were more than mere objects and tales; they were testaments to our intertwined destinies. With each manuscript rolled and secured, each amulet carefully stowed away, a sense of readiness enveloped us. We were not merely leaving behind a cave; we were stepping out from under the shadow of history into the light of possibility.

A renewed sense of purpose filled me, tempered with the weight of responsibility that came with wielding such ancient magic. But it was a burden shared—a yoke made lighter by two sets of shoulders braced against it.

Beauty and I exchanged a look of mutual understanding—a silent agreement that acknowledged the power we held when united. With one final glance at the cave that had sheltered us and served as a crucible for our growing bond, we turned towards the mouth of the cavern.

The biting cold outside beckoned, carrying with it the sharp, crisp scent of ice and snow—fragrances that spoke of a frozen world locked in time. As we stepped out from under the stone archway that marked the threshold between past and present, I knew we were ready to face whatever lay beyond. The snow crunched underfoot, each step a testament to our resolve in this desolate, icy wilderness.

The frosty air nipped at our skin, but the warmth of determination burned within us. Together, undaunted by what awaited us, we would forge a new path—one carved not by fate or curses but by our own hands, intertwined as surely as our destinies were now bound. The frozen landscape around us seemed to echo our silent promise, the ice and snow glittering with the potential of new beginnings.

Transformation and Revelation

Beauty

After days of relentless travel through the unforgiving frozen wasteland, Eirian and I finally stumbled upon a secluded glade, a hidden sanctuary amidst the ice and snow. We had been searching for a place of solitude, somewhere I could safely embrace my dragon shifter abilities without fear of interruption or danger. The journey had been arduous, the biting winds and frigid temperatures testing our endurance, but our resolve had not wavered.

As we approached the glade, the landscape began to change subtly. The harsh, icy terrain gave way to a small haven where the ancient trees stood tall, their branches adorned with frost that glittered in the moonlight. The glade was a striking contrast to the desolation that surrounded it, a serene oasis cradled by the harsh wilderness.

We stepped into the glade, the air noticeably warmer, a gentle reprieve from the biting cold. The moonlight cascaded through the gaps in the ancient trees, pooling around our feet and casting the water before us into a tapestry of silver and shadow. Each leaf seemed to hold its breath, and even the night creatures stilled, as if the forest itself recognized the gravity of what I was about to do.

The glade was a hidden gem, cradled by the frozen wasteland that had become my world. Moonlight cascaded through the gaps in the ancient trees, pooling around my feet and casting the water before me into a tapestry of silver and shadow. Each leaf seemed to hold its breath, and even the night creatures stilled, as if the forest itself recognized the gravity of what I was about to do.

I stepped closer to the edge of the pool, my boots crunching softly on the frost-covered grass. The reflection that stared back at me was a girl on the cusp of becoming something... more. My heart hammered against my ribs, a frantic rhythm in the stillness of the night.

"This is it," I whispered to my reflection, which seemed to quiver with the same mix of emotions that roiled within me. "I have to trust in myself and my powers. There's no turning back."

My hands trembled slightly as I reached for the amulet around my neck—the key to unlocking what lay dormant inside me. It felt warm against my skin, pulsing with an energy that mirrored the steady beat of my heart. With a deep breath, I straightened my shoulders, casting off the cloak of doubt that had settled over me since I first learned of my heritage.

Eirian's presence behind me was a silent source of strength. Though he said nothing, I felt his gaze—an unwavering beacon in a sea of uncertainty. The thought that he believed in me, despite his own struggles and pain, ignited a flame of courage within my chest.

The moon seemed to shine brighter as I closed my eyes and focused on the heat emanating from the amulet. My body grew warm, almost feverish, as if responding to an unseen call. The whispers of transformation echoed in my mind—a promise of wings unfurled and fires kindled from within.

I felt myself swaying slightly, caught in the embrace of an ancient dance that beckoned me to let go. To become who I was meant to be.

With one last glance at Eirian—whose eyes held both fear for me and an unspoken pride—I let the power surge forward. And as it did, I stepped into destiny's outstretched arms, ready to embrace whatever lay beyond.

The air crackled with a palpable energy, an electric hum that vibrated through the very marrow of my bones. My heart pounded, each beat a drum of war, signaling the imminent clash between my human fears and the dragon's might within. The ground beneath my feet shivered, as if the earth itself was wary of the power I was about to unleash.

I closed my eyes, drawing in a deep, steadying breath. Within me, a storm brewed—a tempest of fire and ice, scales and skin, mortal and immortal. It was a struggle as old as time, the eternal dance of duality that now raged within my soul. "Can I really control this power?" I wondered silently. "What if I lose myself to the beast?"

My face twisted in concentration, muscles tensing as I sought to tap into the lineage that flowed like molten gold through my veins. The glow from the amulet around my neck intensified, casting a halo of light that enveloped me in its embrace. The pain came then—a searing agony that felt as though it sought to rend me apart from the inside.

Yet amidst the maelstrom of transformation, there was a whisper of something else—something pure and untamed. It called to me, beckoning me to rise above the pain and fear. I gritted my teeth against the onslaught, refusing to succumb to the doubts that clawed at my mind.

I remembered Eirian's words then, his voice a steadfast anchor in the chaos: "You are more than you know. Your strength lies not in suppressing what you are but in embracing it." His belief in me flickered like a beacon through the fog of my trepidation.

My body began to glow with an ethereal luminescence, casting strange shadows on the trees around me. The transformation was not just physical; it was an awakening—a realization that what I was becoming was not a monster but a testament to heritage and power long forgotten.

I felt it then—the first stirrings of change. It began deep within, a primal force unfurling its wings within the confines of my human shell. There was no turning back now; I had crossed the threshold into the unknown. With Eirian's silent encouragement bolstering my courage, I surrendered to the ancient call of my ancestors.

The dragon's heart within me beat with fierce determination as I embraced my destiny, letting go of who I had been and allowing who I was meant to be to emerge from within.

I could feel Eirian's gaze on me, heavy with a mixture of emotions I didn't dare turn around to read. His silence was a testament to the turmoil that churned between us—a fusion of his own fears and the admiration he tried to mask. I knew he wanted to close the distance, to offer a comforting touch or a word of solace, but this was a path I had to walk alone.

The power within me roared like an untamed inferno, eager to break free and reveal its full glory. Yet, as the energy surged, threatening to overwhelm me, I found solace in the steady rhythm of Eirian's breathing behind me. It was as if his very presence anchored me to this realm, reminding me that no matter how far I ventured into the depths of my dragon's heart, he would be here, waiting for my return.

"She's stronger than she knows. I believe in her," I heard him murmur under his breath—a chant meant for both of us. His voice was the calm in my storm, a balm to the searing pain that threatened to split my soul in two. Each syllable was a lifeline, a tether that kept me grounded even as the world seemed to spin out of control.

My skin stretched and shimmered, scales emerging like jewels upon my flesh. The transformation was nothing short of agony and ecstasy intertwined—each new sensation a discovery of what I had been born to become. Pain lanced through me, sharp and unrelenting, but it was matched by a profound sense of rightness, a completion that I had never before felt. And through it all, Eirian's eyes never left me. His hands were balled into fists at his sides, every muscle coiled tight as if he fought his own battle against the instinct to rush forward and shield me from the unknown.

But he stayed put, understanding that this struggle was mine to conquer—that this pain was a rite of passage into a world that had long called out for its missing heir. His restraint spoke volumes about his respect for my journey, his belief in my strength. It was a silent pledge that he would be there, watching over me, but never interfering.

"You can do this, Beauty. I'm here with you," he whispered across the space that separated us—a promise wrapped in hope and laced with fear. His words were more than mere encouragement; they were an invocation of my strength—a reminder that I was not just Beauty from Eldoria but the last scion of a line that had once danced with dragons beneath a moonlit sky. The power of his belief in me surged through my veins, blending with the ancient magic that now coursed through my body.

Eirian's unwavering faith became my lifeline as my body contorted under the strain of transformation. His silent support became the wings upon which my spirit soared, carrying me through the pain and into the embrace of my destiny. With every fiber of my being alight with ancient power, I let out a breath that was not quite human and stepped fully into the fire of rebirth.

The world around me seemed to hold its breath, the very air pulsing with anticipation as the energy that enveloped me reached a crescendo. I felt my form begin to shift, my human body surrendering to the dragon blood that sang through my veins. It was a dance of fire and life, each movement reshaping me from within. My skin shimmered, scales glistening like molten silver under the moon's caress.

"This is incredible," I whispered to myself, a mantra to steady my racing heart. "I can feel the power and the freedom. This is who I am."

The light that radiated from me blazed like a star being born, blinding and pure. It painted the night with strokes of gold and crimson, a tapestry of my transformation unfolding in real-time. And then, as quickly as it had begun, the light receded, leaving me standing tall in my dragon form—a magnificent blend of power and grace.

I was different now; every fiber of my being hummed with a strength I had never known. My wings unfurled behind me, vast and strong enough to challenge the winds themselves. I stretched them out, feeling each muscle flex with a natural ease that belied their newness.

My eyes—once a soft hue of earth—now glowed with a fierce light that cut through the darkness. I turned to Eirian, seeking the anchor of his gaze amidst the storm of emotions that threatened to overwhelm me. What I found in his eyes was more than I could have hoped for: pride and love so profound it felt like coming home.

I took a moment to adjust to this new form, to the power coursing through my veins like liquid fire. It was exhilarating and terrifying in equal measure, but above all, it was liberating. For the first time in my life, I understood what it meant to be truly free—free from doubt, from fear, from the constraints of a world that had never felt like it fully fit.

Eirian stepped forward, his expression awed yet laced with an unspoken understanding of what this moment meant—not just for me but for both of us. "You are magnificent," he breathed out, his voice filled with an emotion too vast to name.

I could only nod in response, my heart racing with a mix of awe and fear as I embraced my true form. In this moment of transformation, I was not just Beauty; I was a dragon shifter with the legacy of centuries flowing through me.

And as Eirian's hand reached out towards me—a gesture filled with tenderness and strength—I knew that together we were unstoppable. With one last look at him and the pride shining in his eyes, I prepared myself for what came next: taking flight into our destiny

The first beat of my wings lifted me higher than I had ever dreamed, and the world below seemed to shrink away. The cool night air rushed past, a symphony of wind that sang to the deepest parts of my soul. I was no longer bound to the earth; I was a creature of the sky, a dragon in full glory.

With each powerful stroke, I rose higher, and the exhilaration that filled me was purer than any joy I'd known as a human. My scales caught the moonlight, turning it into a cascade of shimmering stars that trailed behind me. I felt invincible, untethered from all my past fears and doubts.

"I've never felt so alive," I whispered to the stars. The power within me surged like a river breaking free from an ancient dam. It was mine—this strength, this freedom—it pulsed through my veins with every beat of my heart. "This power... it's part of me. I have to use it wisely."

With a newfound boldness, I dove toward the earth, only to swoop upward at the last moment, performing loops that made my spirit soar as high as my body. The air became a playground, and I was its master, dancing across the heavens with wings that obeyed my every command.

A laugh bubbled up from within me, born of pure delight. As I climbed once more into the embrace of the night sky, I gathered the magic within me and released it in a stream of icy frost. It spiraled outwards in a breathtaking display of power and beauty—a testament to what I had become.

My heart swelled with pride and joy; not just for what I could do, but for what Eirian and I had overcome together. Glancing down at him, our eyes met across the distance—a silent exchange that spoke volumes. He stood there watching me with awe and admiration etched into every line of his face.

"With Eirian by my side," I thought as our gazes locked together in perfect understanding, "we can overcome anything." His presence grounded me even as I embraced the skies—his belief in me lending strength to my wings.

I continued to soar through the air, each movement more confident than the last. The sense of freedom was intoxicating, but it was his steadfast gaze that anchored me to this world—to our shared destiny—and filled me with an unwavering determination to succeed.

And as the cool wind whispered secrets only heard by those who dare to fly, I knew that together, we were boundless.

I descend from the embrace of the night sky, the rush of wind against my scales giving way to a gentle hush as I touch down on the soft grass of the glade. My heart still beats with the thrill of flight, but as I fold my wings and my form shifts back to human, a serene calm washes over me. The cool night air kisses my skin, now void of scales but tingling with lingering magic.

The transformation leaves me breathless, not from exertion, but from a profound sense of fulfillment. Embracing my dragon heritage has unlocked a part of me I never knew existed. "I am more myself now than I have ever been," I think, feeling a swell of confidence that roots me to the earth even as my spirit soars.

Eirian is there before I fully regain my bearings, his eyes alight with something that looks like pride. It's a look I've fought hard to earn—first his trust, then his respect, and now this shared pride in what we've become together. He doesn't speak; he doesn't need to. His presence is a balm to the raw edges of my exhilaration.

"We're stronger together," I say aloud, voicing the truth that has become irrefutable. With these powers, we are a force unto ourselves—capable of facing any challenge that lies ahead. His hand finds mine, warm and reassuring. The contact steadies me, reminds me that I'm not alone in this.

My smile comes easy, unbidden, as bright as the moon above us. It's a smile born from victory over self-doubt and from the knowledge that whatever comes next, we are ready for it. Eirian's hand tightens around mine in silent agreement.

The night is still around us, filled with the sounds of our shared destiny calling. Our journey is far from over; it's only just begun. But standing here with Eirian, our hands clasped and hearts united in purpose and spirit, I feel an unshakeable confidence.

We stand together in the glade—the same place where fear once held sway—and all I feel now is peace. Peace and an unwavering readiness for whatever comes next.

The glade was aglow with a silver sheen, the moonlight casting ethereal shadows that danced upon the ground. It was here, amidst this tranquil tableau, that I felt the full weight of my transformation settle upon my shoulders—a mantle of power and purpose that was both exhilarating and daunting.

"We should inventory our supplies," Eirian suggested, his voice steady but not without a trace of the same anticipation that coursed through my veins. Together, we gathered our scattered belongings, each item a silent testament to the journey we had endured. Potions, scrolls, and the meager remnants of our provisions lay before us—a mosaic of survival and determination.

As I packed away a tattered map, my thoughts turned inward. "We've come so far, and there's still so much to do. But I know we can succeed together." The words were a mantra in my mind, a source of strength as I considered the path ahead. The final leg of our journey loomed before us—a path fraught with unknown dangers and the promise of an end to our quest.

Eirian caught my gaze, his eyes reflecting the moonlight like twin pools of resolve. "What are you thinking?" he asked.

I hesitated for only a moment before voicing my thoughts. "About everything we've faced... about what's still ahead." I let out a breath I hadn't realized I'd been holding. "I believe in us—in what we can accomplish together."

His hand found mine, fingers intertwining in a gesture that spoke volumes more than words ever could. "Then let's make sure we're prepared for whatever comes next," he said with quiet determination.

We discussed strategies late into the night, huddled over maps and notes by the light of a flickering fire. Eirian's knowledge of tactics complemented my intuition, our plans taking shape like pieces of a puzzle falling into place.

As the fire died down to embers, a sense of unity enveloped us. It was more than just camaraderie; it was the bond of two souls united against a common foe—against fate itself. I looked at Eirian, his features softened by the dim light, and felt my heart swell with love and determination.

"No matter what comes," I thought as our hands remained clasped together in silent pledge, "we'll face it together." The night air was cool on my skin, but within me burned a fire no chill could quench—a fire kindled by purpose and fanned by the love that had grown between us.

With dawn's approach whispering promises of new beginnings, we extinguished the last flames and stood up. We were ready to face whatever lay beyond the glade—side by side.

Forged in Ice and Ice

Prince Eirian, the Dragon Beast

The icy wind howled like a banshee as we made our way through the unforgiving landscape. Freya's fortress, a jagged silhouette against the bleak sky, stood as a monument to her malice. Snow crunched underfoot, each step evidence of our resolve. Beauty's breath formed clouds of vapor that danced away into the frigid air, and I couldn't help but admire her courage, this remarkable woman who had thawed my once-impenetrable heart.

"This is it," I murmured to myself, my voice barely audible above the wind. "We've come so far, and now we're facing the endgame. We can't afford to fail." Memories of Freya's cold laughter and icy touch sent shivers down my spine that had nothing to do with the cold. Yet, as I looked at Beauty, her cheeks flushed from the cold, determination set in her eyes, I felt a surge of warmth that no winter could quench.

"We're close now," Beauty said, her voice steady despite the oppressive surroundings. "Just a little further."

I nodded, my jaw set with determination. The weight of what lay ahead pressed down on me with the heaviness of the mountains themselves. Protecting Beauty was more than a duty; it was a need woven into the very fibers of my being.

The snow seemed to deepen with every step we took toward the looming fortress. My senses were on high alert; I knew all too well the kind of creatures Freya could summon to her defense. Yet even as we advanced into what could very well be a trap, I felt an unwavering resolve solidify within me.

As we traversed this desolate expanse, I glanced at Beauty and found her gaze on me—a gaze filled with trust and something deeper, something that made me feel both vulnerable and invincible at once.

"Are you ready for what comes next?" I asked her, needing to hear her say it.

"I am," she replied without hesitation. "Together."

Her simple affirmation bolstered my spirit like a banner unfurled against the storm. The fortress grew larger now, its icy spires stabbing at the heart of the sky. There was no turning back.

"We'll face whatever comes," I promised her—and myself—as we continued our approach. "Together."

The wind's icy fingers clawed at my cloak as we stood before the ice bridge, its fragile arch the only passage to Freya's looming fortress. Beauty's gaze was fixed on the structure, a mixture of awe and trepidation in her eyes. I could feel the drumbeat of my own heart, rapid against the stillness of the frozen expanse.

"One wrong step and it's over," I thought, studying the treacherous path ahead. The bridge was a skeletal finger, crafted from winter's harshest whispers, and it beckoned us with a deceptive promise of solidity.

"Take it slow," I whispered to Beauty, my voice a steady anchor in the gusting wind. "We can do this."

We walked onto the bridge in unison, our boots pressing into the snow-dusted ice. With each cautious step, I felt the bridge give a mournful groan, as though lamenting its role in this perilous journey. Beneath us, cracks webbed out like dark veins, a stark contrast to the pristine surface.

I kept my gaze forward, but my senses were alert to Beauty's presence beside me. The bond between us had grown stronger than the ice beneath our feet, and it was that strength I clung to now.

A sudden shudder rippled through the bridge, and without thinking, my hand shot out to steady Beauty. My fingers wrapped around her arm with a firmness born of fear and the fierce desire to protect her. She looked up at me, her eyes reflecting both gratitude and resolve.

"We're halfway across," she said, her breath forming crystalline clouds that shimmered before dissipating into the biting air.

I nodded, but my focus remained on the path ahead. The fortress was closer now; its spires appeared sharper against the backdrop of the pale sky. Each step we took was a silent battle against doubt and the elements themselves.

As we moved, I couldn't help but marvel at how far we'd come—together. From mistrust to an unspoken understanding that had become our unbreakable alliance. And as we edged further across that ice bridge, every moment was evidence of our shared determination.

"Just a little further," I urged softly, though whether it was for her benefit or mine, I wasn't sure. Our journey had been one of many trials, but this crossing felt like more than just a physical challenge—it was a crossing into our destiny.

And with each step, we defied the odds stacked against us by fate and Freya alike.

As they neared the fortress, Eirian's senses were on high alert. The air seemed to crackle with an ominous energy, and he could feel the hairs on the back of his neck stand on end. He tightened his grip on his sword, prepared for any ambush that might come their way. His suspicions were confirmed when the very statues lining the path ahead suddenly sprang to life, their frozen forms shattering as they revealed themselves to be icy guardians hell-bent on stopping their progress.

"Beauty, stay close to me!" he called out, his voice a mixture of command and concern. There was no time for pleasantries or small talk as they were immediately engulfed in a flurry of movement and sound. Eirian's sword sang through the frigid air, clashing against the guardians' icy weapons with a chilling ring. His heart pounded in his chest, both from exertion and determination. They couldn't afford to be slowed down now; they were so close to facing Freya and breaking her curse once and for all.

Their enemies pressed in from all sides, but Eirian found solace in the fact that he wasn't alone in this fight. Beauty fought by his side with a ferocity that both impressed and unnerved him. Her dragon heritage shone through as she wielded her staff like an extension of her own body, weaving intricate patterns of fire and ice that left their foes reeling. The synchronization of their movements was uncanny, as if they had been fighting together for years rather than mere weeks.

After dispatching the last of Freya's minions, we paused for a moment, catching our breaths in the eerie stillness that followed. The battle had been fierce, each clash of swords and burst of magic a reminder of the stakes at hand. I looked over at Beauty, her face set with determination, her eyes mirroring the urgency I felt. We couldn't afford to let our momentum falter.

"We can't let them slow us down," I muttered, my voice barely more than a breath amidst the echoing silence of the icy corridors.

Beauty nodded, her resolve unwavering. With a silent agreement, we continued our stealthy advance through the labyrinthine fortress, every step purposeful and measured. The path twisted and turned, leading us deeper into the heart of Freya's domain, each shadow and corner potentially hiding new dangers.

Nestled within the shadow of an ancient, gnarled tree, we found a hidden spot—a natural alcove formed by twisted roots and draped with moss. The air was still, the silence broken only by the distant, muffled chants of Freya's minions patrolling her fortress. I could see the eerie glow of magical wards casting an unnatural light over the jagged ice walls, creating a chilling tableau of power and dread.

"We have to be smart about this," I murmured to Beauty, my voice barely above a whisper. "Freya's powerful, and her minions won't hesitate to kill us." My hands moved with practiced precision, checking the sharpness of my sword's blade and the sturdiness of its hilt.

Beauty nodded, her face set in a determined grimace as she too inspected her gear—a staff imbued with ancient magic that shimmered with a faint light. I watched as she fastened her cloak tightly around her shoulders, steeling herself against the biting cold and whatever horrors awaited us within those walls.

"We've come too far to fail now," I said, my gaze locked with hers. In her eyes, I saw not only the reflection of the fortress's ominous glow but also the fire of conviction that had brought us to this precipice. Her strength bolstered my own, lending me a sense of resolve that coursed through my veins like liquid steel.

Her nod was all the reply I needed—her trust in me unwavering despite the uncertainty that lay ahead. "We've got this," I whispered, more to myself than to her. But it was true; together, we had faced trials that would have broken lesser souls.

I glanced back at the fortress, taking in its towering spires and impenetrable gates. "Once we breach those walls," I began, outlining our strategy once more, "we stick together. No heroics—just keep moving and stay alive." The plan was simple yet fraught with peril; we would need every ounce of our combined skill and cunning to survive.

Beauty's hand found mine for a brief moment—her grip firm and reassuring. It was a silent pact between us—a promise that we would face whatever came next side by side.

The stakes were higher than they'd ever been; not just our lives hung in the balance but also the fate of an entire kingdom cursed by eternal winter. "We have to be smart about this," I thought again as we readied ourselves for what might be our final battle. "Freya's powerful... but so are we."

The icy gates loomed before us, a fortress of solitude that held the heart of our adversary, Queen Freya. My palms were slick against the hilt of my sword as Beauty and I crouched in the shadows, our breaths misting in the frigid air.

"We're in," I thought again, allowing myself that small acknowledgment of victory. "Now the real challenge begins." My gaze flickered to Beauty once more, finding reassurance in her steady presence beside me.

We were two against an empire of frost and fury—but together, we were a force that even Freya would reckon with. And with each step forward, we were rewriting our fates, defiantly carving a path toward freedom and redemption for us all.

The darkness of the fortress's inner sanctum was a living thing, a cloak woven from shadow and malice that seemed to pulse with the beat of dark magic. My heart hammered against my ribs, each thud echoing the growing tension that twisted inside me. Beauty's hand was a steady presence at my back, her touch a silent reminder that we were in this together.

I kept my eyes peeled, scanning every crevice and corner. "Every step brings us closer to Freya. We have to stay sharp," I reminded myself. The corridors were a maze designed to disorient and trap the unwary. But I wasn't just wary—I was ready.

A faint click sounded beneath my boot, and I froze. With a flick of my wrist, I deployed a thin blade from my gauntlet, wedging it into a seam in the wall. A dart shot out from a hidden port, harmlessly clinking off the metal and falling to the stone floor.

"We're almost there," I whispered to Beauty, feeling her nod in response behind me. The confidence in her stance bolstered my own resolve. She had grown so much since we'd started this journey—her strength was now an anchor for my own.

A soft hum of magic grew louder as we approached what could only be described as the heart of Freya's castle. My eyes narrowed as I studied the intricate pattern of runes etched into the floor ahead—a trap, no doubt designed to unleash something unspeakable upon those foolish enough to step carelessly.

I glanced back at Beauty, signaling with a nod toward the ceiling where a crystal glowed faintly with imbued power. She understood immediately, her own knowledge of arcane symbols coming to the fore as she began chanting under her breath—a counter-spell to neutralize the threat.

The crystal dimmed, and the hum faded into silence. We stepped over the now inert runes and continued our careful advance through the labyrinthine corridors.

Every fiber of my being was on edge, but there was also an exhilarating clarity that came with such focus. This place sought to unnerve us with its whispers of power and dominance, yet here we were—a dragon shifter and a cursed prince—challenging an Ice Queen in her own domain.

"We have to stay sharp," I thought again, each word a mantra against the fear that clawed at the edges of my mind. With every silent step and every breath we took, we drew closer to our nemesis and one step nearer to breaking the curse that bound us all.

The frigid air inside Freya's fortress was thick with tension, a silent prelude to the inevitable clash that awaited us. My senses were heightened, every creak and whisper of movement a potential threat. We'd slipped past Freya's guards with a combination of stealth and speed, honed by our shared determination to reach the heart of this icy stronghold.

As we navigated through the labyrinthine corridors, I couldn't shake the feeling of being watched, a prickling at the back of my neck that signaled we were far from alone. Beauty moved beside me, her presence a comforting constant amidst the uncertainty. We were a team, our strengths complementing each other in ways I'd never imagined.

The first wave of Freya's minions emerged from the shadows, their forms materializing from the very ice that encased the fortress. My heart thundered in my chest, a drumbeat of adrenaline and resolve. "We can do this," I whispered to myself, a silent vow that I would protect Beauty at all costs.

Our enemies surged forward, a tide of frost and fury. I met them head-on, my blade singing as it cut through the air. Each clash of steel reverberated through me, a tangible reminder of the battle we'd chosen to fight. Beside me, Beauty's magic flared, a brilliant counterpoint to the darkness that sought to overwhelm us.

I struck with precision, my movements a dance of deadly grace. Every swing, every parry, was for her—to keep her safe and ensure our mission's success. I felt the weight of my responsibility, as tangible as the hilt of my sword clenched tightly in my hand.

In the midst of the chaos, our eyes met, and I saw in hers a mirror of my own resolve. A silent pledge passed between us, strengthening our bond and fueling our determination. "We're in this together," I said, my voice steady despite the maelstrom that raged around us.

Beauty's dragon fire roared to life, a searing tide that melted the ice beneath our enemies' feet, causing them to falter and slide. I seized the momentary advantage, driving my sword into the heart of the onslaught, my actions guided by a singular focus.

The battle raged on, yet amidst the frenzy, there was an undeniable beauty in our coordination. We were two against many, but our unity made us a formidable force. With each fallen foe, we grew more in sync, our actions a seamless blend of power and grace.

Through the clash of swords and the crackle of magical energy, I held onto the belief that we could emerge victorious. We had prepared for this moment, honing our skills and our bond. I was no longer the cursed prince, alone and tormented. I was a warrior, fighting alongside the woman who had breathed new life into my fractured soul.

"I have to protect Beauty and keep her safe," the thought echoed in my mind, a mantra that drove me forward. Each time I looked into her eyes, I found a renewed surge of energy and purpose. I knew that together, we could face whatever challenges Freya's fortress held in store for us.

As the last of the minions fell, a brief silence enveloped us, a calm before the storm we knew was yet to come. I stood by Beauty's side, my breath steady, my resolve unshaken. We had faced the first test of our infiltration and emerged triumphant, our spirits unbroken and our commitment to our cause unwavering.

The battle had begun in earnest, and as we caught our breaths and prepared to venture deeper into the heart of Freya's domain, I knew that we were ready for whatever lay ahead. With every step, we were rewriting our fates, defying the odds, and moving ever closer to our destiny.

Bloodied Ice

Prince Eirian, the Dragon Beast

The throne room loomed before us, a cavernous space that seemed to pulse with a chilling heartbeat of its own. Ice crept up the towering walls, casting jagged shadows that danced eerily in the flickering torchlight. At the far end, Freya, the Ice Queen herself, sat upon her throne—a sculpture of frost and malice—smiling with a coldness that outmatched her frozen domain.

I felt a surge of anger boiling within me as I stared at her, the architect of my torment. The weight of the sword in my hand was a familiar comfort, and I gripped it tighter, ready to unleash years of pent-up fury. "She's caused so much suffering. It ends here, today," I promised myself.

Beauty stood beside me, her eyes ablaze with a fierce determination that mirrored my own. Our journey had forged an unbreakable bond between us—a bond that was about to be tested in the fires of battle.

Freya rose from her throne with a grace that belied her venomous nature. "Welcome, nephew," she sneered, her voice echoing through the icy hall. "And you've brought company. How touching."

"We are here to end your reign of terror," I declared, my voice resounding with a conviction that felt both foreign and empowering.

Freya's laugh was a chilling sound that seemed to freeze the very air around us. "Do you truly believe you can defeat me? You, a cursed beast, and this... girl?"

Beauty's hands clenched at her sides, and I sensed her resolve harden like steel. "This is the moment we've been fighting for," she said through gritted teeth. "I can't let her win. I won't let her hurt Eirian or our people anymore."

Freya's mocking gaze shifted between us. "You think love can save him?" she asked, each word dripping with disdain.

"Yes, I do. And I will prove it," Beauty shot back, unwavering in her stance.

The tension in the room was palpable—a tangible force that seemed to squeeze the breath from my lungs. But as Beauty's voice rang out clear and strong, defiance incarnate against Freya's cruelty, I knew we were ready to face whatever came next. Together.

We stood united in our resolve as Freya descended from her throne, the air growing colder with each step she took toward us. My heart raced with anticipation; every nerve was alight with the knowledge that the final battle was upon us.

With a flourish of her hand, Freya summoned an icy wind that swirled around the room, whipping at our clothes and hair. Yet even as the gale howled its fury and threatened to chill us to our very souls, we did not waver.

"This ends now," I proclaimed, stepping forward to meet my fate alongside Beauty—the woman who had shown me what it truly meant to be brave.

The air crackled with the ferocity of a brewing storm as Beauty and I squared off against Freya in her ice-encrusted throne room. My heart thundered in my chest, pounding out a rhythm of both fear and fierce determination. This was the moment everything had been leading up to, the crescendo in our symphony of rebellion.

I could feel the weight of my ancestral blade in my hand—a sword forged by dragon fire, its mere presence evidence of the power that ran through my veins. As Freya's icy magic swirled around us, I raised my weapon high, a beacon of defiance against her oppressive chill.

"We can't give up," I whispered to myself, my voice drowned out by the clamor of our clashing powers. "We have to win. For our future, and for everyone who's suffered because of her."

Beside me, Beauty's eyes shimmered with the same resolve that fueled my every move. Her dragon magic danced with mine, a tempest of fire that challenged the frostbitten air. We were a force to be reckoned with, our bond a source of unimaginable strength.

Freya's laughter echoed through the chamber, a cruel sound that seemed to mock our struggle. Yet, as she hurled her wintry assaults at us, I knew that her confidence was nothing more than a façade. She had underestimated us—our unity, our love, and the unyielding will that comes from having everything to lose.

With a swift movement, I lunged forward, my sword slicing through the air, meeting Freya's barrage of icy projectiles. Each strike was calculated, my body moving with a precision honed by years of training under the tutelage of some of the kingdom's finest warriors. But this was unlike any battle I had faced before; this was personal.

Beauty's voice cut through the chaos, steady and unwavering. "We're in this together," she declared, her magic surging forth to form a protective barrier around us.

I nodded, my response barely audible over the cacophony. "We can do this. Together."

Our movements were synchronized, a testament to the countless battles we had fought side by side. For every advance Freya made, we had a counter. Our combined power was a spectacle to behold—fire clashing against ice, light piercing through darkness.

The strain of the battle began to take its toll, each spell and parry sapping our energy. Yet, with every successful strike, a spark of hope ignited within me. We were pushing her back, slowly but surely chipping away at her glacial fortress.

As Freya summoned a monstrous wave of ice to crash down upon us, Beauty's eyes met mine, conveying a silent promise. We would not falter. With a ferocious roar, I channeled every ounce of my dragon's fire, melting the wave before it could engulf us.

The room trembled under the force of our magic, the battle reaching a fever pitch. Beauty's dragon form shimmered into existence beside me, her scales glistening like molten gold. Together, we were an unstoppable force, our combined might enough to challenge the very elements.

The clash of our magic reverberated through the frigid air, a symphony of destruction that had Freya's icy fortress trembling at its foundations. My heart beat in time with the rhythm of our spells, each pulse proof of the unyielding resolve that had carried Beauty and me this far.

Yet, as we pressed our advantage, Freya's laughter pierced the cacophony, a sound so chillingly triumphant that it momentarily stilled my soul. "Eirian," she called out, her voice slicing through the chaos with preternatural clarity, "do you truly believe your love for this girl can shatter the curse?"

I tightened my grip on my ancestral blade, the same blade that had been passed down through generations of my family. "I believe in more than just the power of love," I retorted, my voice steady despite the uncertainty that gnawed at me. "I believe in us."

Freya's eyes glinted with malice as she began to circle us, her movements fluid and predatory. "Then allow me to enlighten you, nephew," she said, her words dripping with condescension. "The curse I cast upon you is bound by the ancient magic of our lineage—a magic older than time itself. It cannot be undone by mere mortal affection."

A cold dread began to seep into my bones, a stark contrast to the fiery determination that had burned within me moments before. "What are you saying?" I asked, my voice barely above a whisper.

Freya spread her arms wide, her smile widening as she delivered her crushing blow. "Even if you were to win here today, the curse will endure. Your transformation into the beast is permanent. Your human form, your chance at a normal life—it is all lost to you."

The world seemed to tilt on its axis as her words sank in. Could it be true? Had all our sacrifices been for naught? I felt Beauty's hand on my arm, her touch a lifeline in the storm of my confusion.

"Eirian, look at me," she urged, her voice cutting through the fog of despair that threatened to engulf me. Her eyes, a vibrant shade of green that reminded me of the verdant forests of my homeland, were filled with a resolve that belied her tender years. "We will find a way. Together."

I nodded, the ghost of a smile tugging at the corners of my lips. Her faith in us was unshakeable, and in that moment, I realized that her love was the most potent magic of all.

With renewed vigor, I charged at Freya, my sword clashing against her ice magic with a fury that was born of heartache and hope. Beauty fought beside me, her dragon magic flaring brightly as she summoned a wave of fire to counteract Freya's relentless assault.

But Freya was not yet defeated. With a wave of her hand, she sent a shard of ice hurtling towards us. I pushed Beauty out of the way, taking the brunt of the attack. The impact sent me sprawling, pain lancing through my side.

The world around me spun wildly as Freya's icy spell struck true. I felt the searing pain of the wound, a deep gash that seemed to sear through my very soul. I stumbled, the cold embrace of the ground rising up to meet me as my strength waned. The taste of iron flooded my mouth, each ragged breath a struggle against the encroaching darkness.

I had faced many trials throughout my life, but none as harrowing as the thought of leaving Beauty alone in this frozen wasteland, with Freya's malevolent gaze ever watching. The possibility of her facing the Ice Queen's wrath without me by her side filled me with a fear deeper than any I had ever known.

"Eirian!" Beauty's voice was a lifeline in the swirling chaos of the battlefield. I felt her presence beside me, her warmth a stark contrast to the biting cold of the ice. Her hands, glowing with a radiant light, hovered over my wound, her magic seeking to mend the damage that had been wrought.

"I can't leave her," I whispered to myself, the words little more than a faint murmur. "Not now. We're so close."

My vision dimmed, the edges of my sight growing dark and hazy. I reached out, my fingers brushing against Beauty's. In that fleeting touch, I saw the resolve in her emerald eyes, a determination that mirrored my own. I knew then that she would not abandon our quest, even if I were to succumb to my injuries.

Through the fog of pain, I heard her plea, laden with emotion and fear. "Stay with me, Eirian," she implored, her voice trembling yet filled with an unwavering resolve.

I mustered the last of my strength, my words a quiet promise. "I'm here," I murmured, my hand weakly reaching up to touch her face. The connection between us, forged through trials and tribulations, was the beacon of hope that I clung to in the face of despair.

As Beauty worked her magic, the harsh clash of our surroundings faded into the background. All that existed in that moment was the two of us, bound by a love that had transcended curses and the machinations of a vengeful queen.

The glow from Beauty's hands intensified, casting an ethereal light upon the icy landscape. The stark contrast between the crimson stain spreading across the ice and the radiant energy emanating from her palms served as a poignant reminder of the life-and-death struggle that unfolded around us.

With each passing second, my heart ached with the fear of leaving her behind. The thought of not being there to protect her, to see our journey through to its end, was unbearable. But as I locked my gaze with hers, I found solace in the unwavering love that shone in her eyes—a love that had the power to heal wounds and mend broken hearts.

"I can't lose him," I heard her thoughts echo my own, a silent mantra that resonated within the depths of my soul. Her fear was a mirror of my own, a shared dread that threatened to consume us both.

Yet, in the midst of the turmoil, a sense of peace washed over me. I had no regrets, for I had known the warmth of her love, the strength of her courage, and the beauty of her spirit. Together, we had faced the impossible, and though the path forward was shrouded in uncertainty, I knew that our bond was unbreakable—a force that not even the darkest magic could sever.

"Stay with me, Eirian," she urged once more, her voice a soothing melody amidst the cacophony of battle.

"I'm here," I whispered, my words a testament to the enduring connection that bound us together. In that moment, I understood that as long as our hearts beat as one, hope was never truly lost.

As I lay on the ice, the cold seeping into my bones, I watched Beauty rise with a fierce determination that took my breath away—or perhaps that was the wound Freya had inflicted. Blood pooled beneath me, a stark contrast to the purity of the snow, and yet, it was Beauty's emerald eyes, alight with dragon fire, that held my attention.

"She's incredible," I whispered to the void, my voice barely a rasp. "I've never seen such strength. Please, Beauty, you can do this."

The air around us crackled with the force of her magic. Beauty stood between me and certain death, her body a conduit for the ancient power of her dragon shifter lineage. Her hands glowed with a radiant light, the raw energy of her magic swirling around her like a tempest.

Then Freya, with a wave of her hand, and Beauty was gone. The world went dark.

Reborn Through Love

Beauty

I stepped through the towering archway into Freya's castle, and every instinct within me screamed danger. Just moments ago I was bending over Eirian. Now I was back at the entrance.

The air was a tangible presence, a cold, suffocating blanket of malevolent magic that clawed at my throat with icy fingers. Shadows danced upon the stone walls, their movements a sinister ballet that set my heart to racing. Yet, beneath the fear that threatened to overwhelm me, there was a core of iron resolve, forged in the fires of love and the desperate need to save Eirian.

"Freya!" My voice sliced through the stillness, resonating off the high, vaulted ceiling with a defiance I didn't fully feel. I had to believe that the strength of my voice was a reflection of the power within me—the power of a dragon shifter, the last heir of an ancient lineage.

She materialized before me, her form as cold and sharp as the icicles that hung from the castle's ramparts. Freya's eyes, an icy blue, flickered with contempt as she regarded me. "You think love can save him?" Her voice was a glacial wind, chilling me to the bone.

Anger flared within me, a hot coal that refused to be extinguished by her mockery. My hands curled into fists at my sides. I met her frigid gaze with my own, one that burned with the fire of my conviction. "Yes, I do!"

Her laughter was brittle, shattering the silence like glass upon stone. But as our confrontation unfolded, I listened—not just to her words, but to the undercurrents beneath them. Each taunt, each sneer, was a piece of a larger puzzle. Freya's bitterness was a palpable thing, a twisted, gnarled root that delved deep into the past, into a love that had turned rancid with jealousy and betrayal.

The realization struck me like a bolt of lightning. The curse that bound Eirian, turning him into a beast, was born of hate—a perverse, warped shadow of what love should be. It was a revelation that might have shaken me, had I not been so grounded in the truth of my own heart.

My thoughts raced as I stood before her. "You're wrong, Freya. Your curse is strong, but it's no match for the love that Eirian and I share. It's pure, and it's more powerful than any magic you wield."

Freya's eyes narrowed, a flicker of uncertainty crossing her features. But it was quickly replaced by a mask of indifference. "We shall see, dragon heir. We shall see." And with a wave of her hand, she disappeared.

I could feel the weight of the moment, the significance of the challenge before me. I was no longer just a girl from a cursed village; I was the embodiment of hope, the last glimmer of light in a world blanketed by Freya's eternal winter. I had come too far, endured too much, to falter now. With Eirian's love as my shield and the fire of my dragon's heart as my sword, I was ready to end this.

The air between us crackled with tension, a silent storm that promised destruction and rebirth in its wake. This was the moment we had been fighting for, the culmination of our journey. I would not—could not—let her intimidate me. For Eirian, for our kingdom, I would face whatever trials lay ahead.

As I stood there, the weight of our struggle pressing down on me, my mind wandered back to the moments that had led me to this icy fortress. I remembered the first time I saw Eirian in his beastly form, the fear that had gripped my heart, quickly replaced by a sense of understanding, of kinship. I thought of the laughter we had shared, the quiet conversations by the fire, and the strength we had found in each other. Each memory was a thread, weaving a tapestry of love that now enveloped me with a warmth that belied the frigid air of Freya's domain.

Tears threatened to spill from my eyes as I thought of Eirian, of the pain he had endured, the loneliness that had been his only companion before our paths crossed. I could almost feel the phantom touch of his clawed hand brushing against mine, a gesture that spoke volumes in the silence that often stretched between us. It was a testament to the bond we had forged, a bond that transcended the physical and delved into the very essence of our souls.

I brushed the tears away with the back of my hand, a determined fire igniting within me. I would not let Freya's curse be the end of our story. There had to be a way—a way to free Eirian from the chains of ice that bound him.

And then, like the soft glow of dawn piercing through the darkest night, it came to me. I remembered my mother's voice, the timbre of it a soothing balm to my weary spirit as she recounted tales of old. One story in particular surfaced from the depths of my memory, a tale of a curse that could only be lifted by the purest form of love—true love's kiss.

My breath hitched in my throat as the realization washed over me. "It's the kiss," I whispered to the silent, watching walls. "Our love is true and pure—this is our chance." A surge of hope coursed through my veins, and I felt a renewed sense of purpose. The answer had been within me all along, as simple and as complex as the love I felt for Eirian.

My eyes, which had been clouded with tears mere moments ago, now shone with a fierce determination. I knew what had to be done. I would confront Freya once more, and this time, I would not falter. I would not be swayed by her taunts or her icy glare. I would stand tall, armed with the knowledge that our love was the key to unlocking Eirian's salvation.

With a deep breath, I steadied myself, drawing on the well of strength that seemed to be inexhaustible when it came to protecting those I loved. I had faced dark forests, treacherous rivers, and fire-breathing beasts. I had discovered my true heritage and embraced the power that coursed through my veins. And now, I would face the greatest challenge of all—to break a curse with nothing more than the power of a kiss.

A kiss that was more than just a fleeting touch of lips; it was a promise, a vow to stand by Eirian's side, to share in his joys and sorrows, to face whatever trials may come with the steadfast resolve of two hearts beating as one.

I squared my shoulders and took a step forward, the amulet at my neck pulsing with a warm, reassuring light. I was ready to face Freya, to reclaim the future that had been stolen from us. With each step, my resolve hardened, and the words I would speak to her formed in my mind.

The air was thick with the scent of ancient ice and the metallic tang of blood—Eirian's blood. My heart thrummed against my ribcage like a caged bird, each beat a frantic plea for time that was slipping through our fingers. "Hold on, Eirian," I whispered into the icy stillness, my voice steady despite the turmoil within.

The castle seemed to conspire against me, walls shifting and corridors warping as Freya's dark magic sought to impede my progress. But I was undeterred, fueled by a love that burned brighter than any spell she could cast. With the Dragon's Heart pulsing warm against my skin, I pushed forward, slicing through enchanted barriers and evading the malevolent creatures that snarled and clawed at my heels.

Finally, I burst into the cavernous chamber where Eirian lay, his lifeblood staining the pristine white floor. His breaths were shallow, his skin ashen beneath the dark fur of his beastly form. The sight of him like this—broken and bleeding—shattered my heart into a thousand pieces. Yet, even as despair clawed at my throat, I refused to succumb to it.

I fell to my knees beside him, my hands fluttering uselessly above his massive form. "I love you, Eirian," I murmured, my voice laced with the pain of possibly losing him. His eyes, a striking shade of gold, found mine, and in their depths, I saw a reflection of my own soul—a tapestry woven with threads of sorrow, hope, and an unspoken promise of eternal devotion.

Tears blurred my vision as I leaned in, my lips brushing against his in a kiss that was both a prayer and a vow. It was a kiss that carried the weight of our shared journey, the battles we had fought, the love that had blossomed in the midst of darkness and despair. I poured every ounce of my being into that kiss, willing the pure, unyielding love I felt for him to shatter the chains of the curse.

As our lips met, a surge of energy cascaded through the room, a tempest of light and warmth that clashed violently with the surrounding cold. The Dragon's Heart glowed fiercely, its light seeping into Eirian's skin, mingling with the magic that bound him. I felt the moment the curse began to unravel—a sensation like the first, tentative rays of the dawn sun piercing through the night sky.

I felt it then—the tremor that traveled from the soles of my feet, up through the core of my being. The air around us shimmered like heat from a desert sun, magic saturating the frosty atmosphere of Freya's lair. It was as though a silent bell had rung, its vibrations the herald of profound change. I watched, hardly daring to breathe, as the first fissures appeared in Freya's icy facade, her dominion fracturing beneath the onslaught of a greater, purer love.

Eirian's body, still locked in the monstrous form of the beast, convulsed. My heart clenched, not from fear but from the burgeoning hope that blazed brighter with each passing moment. His golden eyes, wild and brimming with untold stories, held mine captive as the transformation commenced. It was like witnessing the dawn, light breaking over the darkness of an endless night, warmth spreading across a realm entombed in perennial winter.

Layer by layer, the beast's visage began to dissolve. My breath caught in my throat as his form shifted and shrank, scales retreating to reveal alabaster skin that bore the faint tracery of the dragon lineage that flowed through his veins. His eyes remained a vivid gold brown, vibrant and alive in a way they hadn't been before. A silent tear slipped down my cheek as I beheld him, fully restored and resplendent in the golden glow of the Dragon's Heart.

"It's working," I whispered, more to myself than anyone else. "He's coming back to me." My voice wavered, and I clung to the truth that settled in my bones with an unshakeable conviction—we had done it. The curse that had shrouded Eirian's life in darkness was lifting, powerless against the tide of our shared love.

As the last traces of the curse vanished into the ether, Eirian took a deep, unsteady breath. It was the sound of liberation, the awakening of a man reborn. Our eyes met, and in his gaze, I saw my own joy reflected a hundredfold. "Eirian," I managed to say, my heart feeling too large for my chest, brimming with an unspeakable love that threatened to burst forth in a thousand unspoken words

A sob of relief escaped my lips as I cradled his face in my hands, our foreheads touching. "You're free," I breathed, the words a balm to my wounded heart. Eirian's arms wrapped around me, pulling me close as we both trembled with the enormity of what had just occurred.

"Beauty," he whispered, the single word a melody that resonated through every fiber of my being. His voice, strong yet filled with a depth of emotion that belied the strength of his body's new form, conveyed the astonishment and gratitude that neither of us had anticipated could truly exist outside of fairy tales and whispered legends.

We sat there for a moment that stretched into eternity, silent yet more eloquent than any grand declaration could ever be. In his eyes, I saw not just the acknowledgment of what had passed between us, but the promise of all the wonders yet to come—wonders that would be written in the bright tapestry of our lives.

With great tenderness, he reached for my hand, threading his fingers through mine. It was a simple gesture, but one weighted with the triumph of our shared victory, our hands becoming the icons of a love so fierce that it had not merely broken a curse but shattered an age-old legacy of malice and despair.

Triumph surged through my veins, not the cold triumph of the conquering hero, but a warm, living exaltation that came from deep within my soul—from the place where fear could not dwell, and darkness held no sway. Eirian was free. And in that liberation, I found the greatest joy of my young life, a joy so complete and all-consuming that it seemed the universe itself could not contain its bounds.

Freya's ice fortress, once an emblem of cold isolation, now crumbled around us, its ruin beautiful and bittersweet—for even in the depths of winter's heart, the wheel of time would turn, heralding the end of an era and the bright, uncharted expanse of a new world order, one built not on fear and bitterness, but on hope and love. Eirian and I were entwined in the vanguard of that brighter future, standing at the threshold of an eternal dawn, our destinies irrevocably linked by the power of the purest kiss imaginable.

Of Freya, there was no trace. She had vanished into the shadows. Yet, I could feel it in my bones—she was not truly gone. Her presence lingered, a haunting echo in the corridors of my mind, promising that this was only a temporary reprieve. The air around me seemed to pulse with the malevolent energy she had left behind, a constant reminder that our battle was far from over. I clenched my fists, my resolve hardening. Freya would return, and when she did, I would be ready.

The curse shattered, the oppressive silence that had once hung heavy in the air was now pierced by the sound of our sobs. Eirian, his eyes a mirror to the sky at dawn, reached for me with hands that spoke of longing and a journey fraught with shadows now dispelled. I fell into his embrace, the solid strength of his arms encircling me like the roots of an ancient tree.

"I thought I lost you," I cried into the fabric of his tunic, my tears soaking into the threads as if to weave our story into its very fibers.

"You saved me," he murmured against my hair, his voice a low rumble that resonated with the beating of my heart. "I love you so much."

The words hung between us, simple yet laden with all the complexities of our intertwined fates. We had traversed realms of fear and uncertainty, had danced on the edge of despair, and yet here we were, bound tighter by every trial that sought to tear us apart.

My hands gripped his back, fingers tracing lines of relief as if I could map out our past and future in one touch. The fear that had clutched at my soul released its icy hold, melting away under the warmth of his skin against mine.

Eirian pulled back just enough to look at me, his gaze holding a universe of emotion. "Beauty," he said, my name a sacred utterance on his lips. It was a vow, a benediction spoken in the silent language of souls that knew each other beyond time and form.

I met his eyes, seeing within them not just Eirian the man, but Eirian the dragon—the noble creature whose wings had been clipped by darkness but now could soar once more. In those eyes, I saw our future unfurling like the first bloom in spring's tender embrace.

"Thank you for coming back to me," I whispered, my voice steady even as tears continued their path down my cheeks. His thumb brushed them away with a tenderness that made my breath catch.

We stood there amidst the remnants of Freya's broken fortress—two hearts that had weathered a storm that would have broken lesser spirits. In this moment of emotional reunion, nothing else mattered but the love that pulsed between us—a love as fierce as dragonfire and as gentle as falling snowflakes.

We didn't need grand declarations or poetic words; our embrace said it all. We were home—in each other's arms—our bond a beacon of light against any darkness that might dare encroach upon our shared destiny again.

As the last vestiges of Freya's curse dissolved into nothingness, the very air around us seemed to sigh in relief. The icy walls of her fortress wept, droplets cascading down like a symphony of renewal, and the frozen ground beneath our feet gave way to a carpet of verdant green. All around us, ice surrendered to the insistent push of life; flowers unfurled their petals as if to greet the sun's warm embrace for the first time in an age.

"We did it," I breathed, my voice barely above a whisper, but Eirian heard me. He pulled back just enough to see my face, his eyes shining with unshed tears and something more—hope.

"Together," he replied, his hand still clasping mine, an anchor in the sea of change.

The transformation of the kingdom unfolded before us like a tapestry being woven by an invisible hand—strokes of color returning to a landscape that had forgotten the hues of spring. It was as if the land itself was waking from a deep slumber, stretching its limbs and basking in the newfound warmth.

From our vantage point, we watched as people emerged from their homes like hibernating creatures tentatively exploring a world reborn. Their voices carried on the wind, a mixture of laughter and incredulous delight painting the air. Children danced in the melting snow, splashing in burgeoning puddles that reflected the cerulean sky above.

Eirian squeezed my hand gently, drawing my gaze back to him. "Look at what you've started," he said with a soft chuckle that rumbled through his chest.

I smiled at him, my heart swelling with an emotion so profound it threatened to spill over. "No," I corrected him gently. "Look at what we've started."

In that moment, as we stood hand in all amidst the crumbling remnants of tyranny and fear, I felt our bond solidify into something unbreakable. We had faced darkness together and emerged not just victorious but transformed. And as we gazed out at the kingdom—the kingdom we would rebuild together—I knew that this was only the beginning.

Around us, life unfurled in a cascade of colors and sounds—the vivid green of new grass poking through snow, the vibrant reds and yellows of flowers waking from their frozen slumber, and above all, the golden light of sunlight breaking through clouds that had lingered too long.

We did it. We brought the light back to our kingdom. And as I stood there with Eirian, our hands clasped together as tightly as our fates, I knew that whatever future awaited us, we would face it together.

The thawing of Eldoria was a spectacle that would have filled any heart with wonder. The once rigid claws of ice released their grip on the land, surrendering to a cascade of water that shimmered with the promise of spring. Yet, as laughter and cheers echoed through the kingdom, a whisper of unease wound its way through the jubilant cries, coiling tightly around my heart.

Eirian stood beside me, his hand clasped in mine, as we watched the transformation. "It's beautiful," he said, his voice tinged with awe. But as I turned to share a smile with him, something flickered at the edge of my vision—a shadow that seemed to move against the natural order of light.

I tightened my grip on Eirian's hand, a silent alert that I had noticed something amiss. He followed my gaze, his eyes narrowing as he too caught sight of the anomaly. There was no mistaking it; something lingered in the shadows.

"It's not over yet," I whispered, the words tasting like ash on my tongue. How I wished they weren't necessary—that we could bask in our victory without fear of what darkness might still be lurking.

Eirian's nod was almost imperceptible, yet it held the weight of a thousand unspoken promises. "We'll face it together," he affirmed, his voice steady and resolute.

In that moment, the air around us seemed to grow colder, as if nature itself had overheard our exchange and paused in anticipation. Then came a sound so faint I thought I might have imagined it—a sinister laugh that danced across the winds from far away.

My eyes met Eirian's once more, and I saw in them the same steely determination that I felt coursing through my veins. This battle may have been won, but our war against the darkness was not yet finished. We had both sensed it—the lingering threat that clung to our shadows like a malevolent specter.

"We have to stay vigilant," I said, my voice barely above a murmur. But there was power there—a conviction forged in fire and tempered by trials that few could fathom.

Eirian's hand gave mine a reassuring squeeze as we stood united amidst the celebration that now felt like a fragile veneer over an unseen abyss. "Then we'll be vigilant," he replied with quiet confidence. "Together."

The crowd around us continued to revel in their newfound freedom, but for Eirian and me, there was no such luxury. We had glimpsed the face of true evil—and we knew all too well that it did not yield easily.

As we exchanged one final look—a silent vow to protect this kingdom and each other from whatever darkness might come—I felt the full weight of our destiny settle upon us. And though the path ahead was shrouded in uncertainty, one thing was clear: we would walk it side by side.

The Heir's Legacy

Beauty

The night had wrapped the castle in a cold embrace, its cool fingers creeping through the cracks of my chamber. I lay in bed, layers of blankets drawn up to my chin, yet the chill was not what kept me from the comfort of dreams. No, it was a restlessness that stirred in my chest—a whispering wind that seemed to call my name with an urgent breath.

I rose, my feet touching the cold stone floor, sending shivers up my legs. The walls were silent sentinels as I draped a thick shawl over my shoulders. It was a deep blue, like the twilight sky just before the stars claim their dominion. The fabric hugged me with a fleeting warmth that did little to fend off the persistent cold.

Why can't I sleep? The question was a silent echo in my mind as I stepped into the shadowed hallway. The castle at night was a different realm—a labyrinth of moonlit stone and deep pockets of darkness where the light dared not tread. I felt an inexplicable pull, an almost instinctual feeling that beckoned me toward a part of this grand structure I rarely visited.

My heart thrummed in my chest, each beat an affirmation of purpose as I passed tapestries that told tales of old. They were lifeless now, their vibrant threads muted in the dim light. Curiosity entwined with an underlying sense of destiny propelled me forward. What secrets lay dormant within these walls? What answers whispered just beyond my reach?

With each step, I felt as though I was unraveling a thread that led to some great unveiling. The air seemed to grow colder still, and I could see my breath—a ghostly apparition dancing before me before dissipating into the darkness.

"Something's calling me," I murmured to myself, barely audible over the sound of my own footsteps. The corridor stretched endlessly before me, and yet it felt as if it were shrinking with each step, guiding me, urging me onward.

A door loomed ahead—tall and unassuming—and yet it drew me like a moth to flame. My hand reached out, fingertips brushing against the rough wood before pressing down on the handle. It creaked open with a groan of protest, revealing an ancient chamber veiled in shadows and mystery.

The night was indeed cold, wrapping the castle in its chill embrace—a chill that mirrored the unease within me. But now, standing at the threshold of discovery, that unease gave way to something else: a burgeoning anticipation for what lay ahead.

The silence of the castle was a shroud that seemed to thicken with each step I took, guiding me away from the familiar warmth of my chambers. I could no longer ignore the pull that tugged at my very soul, leading me down a corridor I had seldom ventured. The air grew colder, whispering secrets of a time long past, and there, beneath the moon's pale gaze through a nearby window, I discovered a tapestry. Its edges were frayed, the image faded—a battle scene, proud and fierce, yet forgotten by those who walked these halls.

My fingers traced the intricate weave, and beneath it, they found an anomaly in the wall. A chill traced my spine as I pushed against the stone; it swung inward with a silent plea to be remembered. Heart pounding like a war drum, I slipped through the opening with nothing but the soft glow of my lantern to guide me.

The chamber beyond was cloaked in shadows and dust—an untouched sanctum where time itself seemed to have halted its relentless march. My breath hung before me, a ghostly sentinel in the lantern's golden light as I stepped further into the hidden room. Scrolls and artifacts lay scattered upon shelves and tables as if left in haste by those who once deemed them precious.

"What is this place?" My voice was barely above a whisper, yet it filled the chamber with the weight of centuries. Here lay knowledge forgotten, wisdom abandoned in the wake of whatever calamity had befallen this place. My fingers hovered over a scroll, its edges yellowed with age, and as I unfurled it with reverent care, words danced before my eyes—tales of dragon shifters and their ancient pacts with kingdoms now lost to legend.

Awe enveloped me as I delved deeper into the trove of history before me. Each artifact told its own story—a chalice still bearing the faint scent of celebratory wine, a dagger whose blade whispered of battles won and lost. It was as if these relics had been waiting for me, for someone who could understand their silent testimony.

The air around me grew heavy with anticipation. Here in this forsaken chamber lay answers to questions I hadn't yet dared to ask. With each breath, each moment spent among these remnants of a bygone era, I felt myself becoming more than what I had been—a bridge between what once was and what might yet be.

I settled onto my knees beside an ornate chest carved with dragons entwined in an eternal dance. My hands shook as they worked at its clasp; it gave way with a sigh of release that echoed through the room like a benediction. Inside lay scrolls sealed with wax emblems that beckoned me closer—a call to unravel their secrets and claim my place within this ancient lineage.

Freya's curse may have lifted from our lands, but she was still around, somewhere. New challenges awaited— challenges that these scrolls might help us overcome. With bated breath and hands that trembled not from cold but from possibility, I reached for them...

I hesitated, my hand hovering above the ancient scroll that lay nestled among the relics of a bygone era. It was adorned with a dragon emblem, fierce and regal, and below it, a family crest that I recognized all too well—it was undeniably tied to my own lineage. My fingers grazed the wax seal, and I felt a tingle of magic spark at my touch. With a deep breath, I broke the seal and unfurled the delicate parchment.

The chamber was silent, save for the soft rustle of the scroll as it revealed its secrets to me. My eyes raced over the cryptic text, each word etched in ink that seemed to have been drawn from the very essence of night. And then I found it—a prophecy that spoke of a dragon heir destined to sway the kingdom's fate on the edge of a blade-thin line: prosperity or destruction.

"A dragon heir... who will either bring prosperity or destruction," I read aloud, my voice an intruder in the hushed sanctum. The words echoed off the stone walls, carrying with them the weight of a destiny I had yet to fully grasp.

Could this be about me? Or our child? The thought clawed at my mind with talons of fear and wonder. I was torn between the awe of potentially fulfilling an ancient legacy and the terror of an ominous future that might await us all. My hands trembled slightly as I held the scroll closer, as if proximity could lend clarity to its foreboding message.

This chamber, hidden away from prying eyes and untouched by time's relentless march, now cradled a truth that could alter our lives irrevocably. The prophecy was clear in its duality but maddeningly vague in its details. What actions would lead to prosperity? What missteps might herald destruction? The questions swirled in my head like leaves caught in an autumn gale.

I wrapped my arms around myself, feeling suddenly very small amid the remnants of history that surrounded me. This prophecy had lain dormant for centuries, waiting for someone of my bloodline to uncover it. But why now? Why me?

I knew not whether to feel honored or cursed—chosen or condemned. With each heartbeat, I felt an undeniable connection to this prophecy, as though it were a thread woven into the very fabric of my being.

"Unparalleled prosperity or devastating destruction," I whispered once more, letting the gravity of those words sink into my bones. Whatever path lay ahead, one thing was certain: our lives were entwined with this ancient prophecy's fulfillment, for better or for worse. And as I carefully rolled up the scroll and tucked it into my satchel, I resolved to face whatever came with courage—courage befitting a dragon heir.

The library's warm glow enveloped me, a stark contrast to the icy dread that clung to my heart. I had carried the ancient scroll through the castle's silent corridors, my arms cradling it as if it were a newborn child—fragile, yet filled with potential. Now, seated at a worn oak table, I unfurled the parchment with trembling hands. My ancestors' notes and translations lay scattered before me, their once-bright ink now faded to a ghostly hue.

"I need to understand this," I murmured to myself, my breath fogging in the air despite the crackling fire nearby. The language was old, cryptic—a tapestry of symbols and metaphors woven by a mind that viewed time and fate as mere threads to be pulled and twisted. I poured over each line, cross-referencing with dusty tomes that creaked open with protest, revealing their secrets grudgingly.

Hours slipped by unnoticed as I delved deeper into the past, my fingers tracing lines of text that spoke of trials by fire and shadow, of allies hidden in plain sight, and enemies with hearts encased in ice. Each revelation was like a puzzle piece clicking into place—a picture slowly forming from the mists of legend and prophecy.

"This isn't just about me," I realized, my voice barely audible in the hush of the library. The weight of history pressed down upon me, as tangible as the scroll in my hands. The prophecy hinted at a dragon heir—someone born of both human and dragon blood—who would face challenges that could shape our very world. Could it be referring to me? Or perhaps to the child I might one day bear?

A knot formed in my stomach as I pondered the implications. The thought of bringing a life into this tangled web of destiny filled me with both awe and terror. Yet as I continued to decipher the ancient words, something within me shifted—a hardening of spirit, a steeling of resolve.

My heritage was not just a gift; it was a call to arms. And whether this prophecy spoke of blessings or calamities yet to come, I knew that I must rise to meet it head-on. For my kingdom's sake. For Eirian's sake. For the sake of the child who might one day look up at me with eyes wide with wonder and ask about their place in this story.

The fire popped and hissed beside me, its sparks ascending like tiny stars seeking their place in the heavens above. And there, amidst the dance of flame and shadow, I found a semblance of peace—a quiet acceptance of the path that lay before me.

With each symbol I deciphered, my sense of dread was slowly replaced by an unwavering determination. This was more than just my battle; it was a legacy centuries in the making—a legacy that I would honor and fulfill, no matter what trials awaited me beyond these ancient walls.

The moment Eirian stepped through the door, I felt the weight of destiny upon us. His gaze met mine, and without a word, he knew. He knew that the silence hanging in the air was laden with a revelation that would forever alter our course.

"Eirian," I started, my voice barely above a whisper, yet carrying the urgency of a drumbeat calling us to war. "There's something you need to see." My hands, surprisingly steady given the turmoil inside me, unfurled the scroll that I had clutched like a lifeline.

His footsteps were measured as he approached, a testament to the control he wielded over his own unease. Leaning over my shoulder, his breath fanned across my cheek as his eyes took in the ancient script—a language that spoke of times when dragons ruled the skies unchallenged.

I watched his expression shift from curiosity to concern as he read, his brow furrowing with each line. The prophecy was cryptic, yet its message rang clear—a dragon heir whose fate would steer our kingdom into light or shadow.

"We have to be ready," I said, my voice steadier now. The scroll seemed to hum with energy between us, its words a harbinger of trials yet to come.

Eirian's hand found mine, his fingers intertwining with mine in silent solidarity. "We will face this together," he said, and there was no mistaking the resolve in his voice—a resolve mirrored in my own heart.

The gravity of what lay ahead settled over us like a mantle. But within that weight, there was also a binding force—a unity forged in fire and strengthened by every challenge we had faced side by side.

As we stood there, hand in hand, I realized that whatever future this prophecy foretold—be it fraught with danger or brimming with hope—we would meet it as one. Together, we were more than just two souls entwined by fate; we were guardians of a legacy that stretched back through the ages.

Our determination was silent but unyielding; it filled the room like a tangible force. And as I gazed into Eirian's eyes—eyes that had seen both the beauty and the terror of this world—I knew that together we could face anything. Our love was our armor, and our will was our weapon.

No words were needed as we shared this moment of understanding. We were united, not just by the love that blossomed in our hearts but also by the shared responsibility that now rested on our shoulders. Whatever came next, we would not falter—we would stand firm and rise to meet it head-on.

Gathering Shadows

Prince Eirian

Back in the hidden chamber, I urged Beauty to take a moment for herself, my hand lingering on her shoulder a heartbeat longer than necessary. Her eyes, wide with the weight of her discovery, met mine and softened. "Rest for a moment," I whispered, my voice barely rising above the hush of the hidden chamber.

She nodded, her hands ceasing their tremble as she sank down onto a stone bench, the glow from the amulet casting dancing lights across her features. I watched her for a second longer, ensuring she was truly alright before turning back to the room that held secrets of our past and perhaps keys to our future.

My gaze swept over the chamber, and it was as if every shadow beckoned with whispers of ancient times. The air was thick with the scent of old parchment and dust, a testament to centuries gone by. I approached a grand tapestry that hung from the wall, its threads depicting battles and triumphs of my ancestors. The intricacies of the woven scene held me captive; it was history made tangible.

Beside it, encased in glass that had somehow remained unscathed by time's cruel hand, lay a family tree. My fingers traced over the cool surface as I read names that resonated with a sense of familiarity yet felt like strangers. "So much history," I thought aloud, my voice echoing slightly in the cavernous space.

A nearby pedestal caught my attention next. Upon it rested battle records – leather-bound volumes that were worn at the edges but still held strong. I flipped through them carefully, each page a canvas of inked strategies and fallen heroes. Pride swelled within me for these warriors of old; they had fought valiantly for our kingdom.

Every so often, I stole glances back at Beauty. She had her eyes closed now, her chest rising and falling in the steady rhythm of sleep.

The concern that had knotted in my chest eased slightly at the sight – she was safe here with me.

"We're in this together," I murmured to myself as I continued my search. It wasn't just about breaking curses or fulfilling prophecies anymore; it was about us, forging a path neither of us could walk alone.

I felt a surge of protective love for her then, stronger than any magic I'd ever known. It fortified me as I delved deeper into our shared legacy, determined to uncover all that we needed to face whatever lay ahead – together.

The stillness of the hidden chamber was like a heavy cloak, wrapping around us with the weight of centuries. I had positioned myself between Beauty and the secrets that spilled out from the dusty tomes and faded tapestry. She needed rest, and I, her vigilant guardian, could afford no reprieve. My gaze flitted across the room, seeking out truths among the relics of our intertwined legacies.

That's when the silence shattered. The door to the chamber groaned open, its protest echoing off stone walls. I moved without thought, stepping in front of Beauty, my hand finding the hilt of my sword as if drawn by a magnet. "Who goes there?" I growled, my voice slicing through the hush.

The figure that emerged from the shadowed threshold caused my grip to loosen ever so slightly, but not my guard. It was an old advisor, one whose wisdom had once been a beacon in my father's court. His eyes held stories long buried, his gait slow but purposeful as he approached us.

Master Cadoc, a man of indomitable presence despite his age, had always been a pillar of strength and knowledge. His hair, now silvered with time, flowed like a river of wisdom. His eyes, deep and piercing, bore the weight of countless secrets and battles fought in the shadows of our history. His robes, though worn, still carried the regal aura of the court, embroidered with symbols of protection and knowledge.

I could feel Beauty stir behind me; her breath hitched in a silent question that hung between us. "Master Cadoc," I acknowledged him with a nod, though my hand remained on my sword, ready to defend against both seen and unseen threats.

He bowed his head in reverence before lifting his gaze to meet mine. "My prince," he began, his voice a whisper of leaves against stone. "The prophecy you've uncovered bears more than just words; it is a map of what was... and what may yet be."

Master Cadoc's eyes shifted to Beauty then back to me as he continued. "There are forces at play that seek to twist fate's threads to their own design." His words were cryptic, yet they bore an urgency that clawed at my insides. His presence here, after so many years of silence, was both a comfort and a warning. The shadows of our past were long, and their reach extended into our future.

Beauty had awakened and stepped beside me now, her presence a calming force despite the storm of emotions brewing within me. Could we trust him? This man who had vanished when darkness fell upon our house? Yet here he stood before us, bearing warnings that could not be ignored.

My suspicion battled with curiosity as he spoke of ancient enemies lurking in shadows, their eyes set upon the throne – upon us. With every revelation, I felt Beauty's resolve strengthen beside me. Her hand brushed against mine, a silent pact forming between us.

Master Cadoc's voice took on a more urgent tone. "You must understand, my prince, my lady, that the prophecy is not a fixed path but a potential one. Your choices, your strength, and your unity can alter the course it predicts." He paused, letting his words sink in. "There are those who would use your strength for ruin, to bend your will to their dark desires."

The flickering candlelight bathed Beauty's study in a warm, golden hue as we settled at the oak table laden with relics of our past. I spread the scrolls and artifacts before us, their edges worn by the touch of time. "Let's make sense of this," I said, my voice a steadfast anchor in the sea of uncertainty that lay ahead.

Beauty leaned forward, her fingers tracing the ancient script with a reverence that spoke of her deep connection to this legacy. I watched her, my heart swelling with a mixture of emotions – admiration for her strength, concern for the burden she shouldered, and a love that had become the very beat of my heart.

"She's so strong," I thought, even as my dragon instincts raged within me, urging me to shield her from the coming storm. But she was not one to be shielded; she was my equal, my partner in every sense.

Our hands brushed against each other as we worked side by side, each touch a silent vow to stand together no matter what darkness we might face. With every connection we pieced together between the prophecy and our ancestors' history, a tapestry of destiny began to unfold.

Yet as we delved deeper into the web of lineage and power, my mind wandered to the shadows that lingered at the edges of our light. The prophecy was clear: great prosperity or devastating destruction would befall the kingdom through the dragon heir. The weight of such an outcome bore down on me, yet it was Beauty's well-being that anchored my concern.

Master Cadoc's presence was a stark reminder of the stakes. His words had painted a picture of a world teetering on the edge, with forces both seen and unseen ready to tip the balance. "We have to be ready," I murmured more to myself than to her. My gaze lifted to meet hers, and I saw the echo of my own determination reflected back at me. Her presence fortified me, lending strength to my resolve as we unraveled the mysteries before us.

Together, we began to map out not just our history but our future – one where every decision we made now could tip the scales for our kingdom. The stakes were higher than ever before, but so too was our unity. As Master Cadoc stood by, his eyes watching our every move, I felt a sense of destiny wrap around us. The path ahead was fraught with peril, but with Beauty by my side and the guidance of wise allies, we would face whatever came our way.

I felt it then – a clarity that cut through doubt like a blade. We were chosen by fate, yes, but it was our choices now that would define its course. With Beauty by my side, there was no trial too great, no enemy too formidable. We were bound by love and purpose, and together we would face whatever lay ahead with unwavering courage.

As I glanced at Beauty once more, her eyes alight with the fire of determination and intellect, I knew that together we were unstoppable. And in that moment, all fear was banished by the promise of what we could achieve side by side.

In the council room, the air hung heavy with the scent of ancient wood and whispered secrets. Beauty and I sat close, our focus drawn to the map that sprawled across the broad table, its edges curling like withered leaves. "We'll need allies," she said, her finger tracing the lines that connected our kingdom to lands beyond.

I nodded, feeling the familiar churn of my thoughts as I considered each name she suggested. "Who can we trust?" The question loomed over us, its answer as elusive as shadows at dusk.

We poured over the list of names, discussing each with a measured deliberation. There were those who had stood by my family through prosperity and peril alike – old alliances forged in the fires of trust. And then there were others, newer bonds tempered by recent trials.

As we spoke, a flicker of hope kindled within me. With the right support, we could face whatever darkness lay ahead. Yet beneath my strategic considerations ran a current of concern for Beauty's safety. It was a constant thrum in my veins, a vow that echoed with every beat of my heart: *I'll protect her, no matter what.*

My hand reached out almost unconsciously, covering hers where it rested on the parchment. Her skin was warm against mine – a touch that spoke of unity and strength. "We'll find the right people," I assured her, my voice steady despite the tempest of thoughts within me.

She smiled then, a soft curve of her lips that held more power than any army I could muster. For a moment, it felt as though our burdens had lightened, as if her smile could fend off the looming threat all on its own.

Our conversation turned to strategies for securing alliances – feasts and treaties, words and promises – but all the while I couldn't shake off that protective instinct. It was as if I could see the battles ahead, hear the clash of steel, feel the heat of dragon fire. And in every vision that played before my mind's eye, there stood Beauty – brave and resolute.

"We must be wise," I murmured, more to myself than to her. "And cautious." The stakes were too high for rash decisions; one misstep could spell disaster not just for us but for all those who called this land home.

Her hand gave mine a gentle squeeze – a silent message of trust and shared resolve. And with that simple gesture, I knew we were ready to face whatever came our way – together.

The heavy oak doors of the council room creaked open, heralding the arrival of our much-anticipated ally. The air was thick with tension, every breath a whisper of the uncertainty that cloaked our future. Beauty stood beside me, her hand resting lightly on the hilt of her sword, a silent testament to her readiness for whatever lay ahead.

Our ally, Lord Carnahorn, entered with measured steps, his eyes sweeping the room before settling on us. He was a formidable figure, clad in armor that had seen many battles, and his presence filled the space with an aura of indomitable strength. I stepped forward to greet him, my heart hammering against my chest. "Lord Carnahorn," I began, "thank you for coming."

He nodded, his gaze piercing as he regarded us both. "Prince Eirian, Lady Beauty," he said in a voice that resonated with authority. "I have heard of your plight and the prophecy that binds your fate to the kingdom's."

I swallowed hard, feeling the weight of our responsibility press down upon me. This was the moment of truth—the chance to secure an alliance that could tip the scales in our favor. With a steadying breath, I laid bare our situation and the critical role of the prophecy.

As I spoke, I watched Lord Carnahorn closely, searching for any sign of his intentions. The silence that followed my words was a living thing, wrapping around us like a shroud. "Will they help us?" The question clawed at my mind, a relentless beast gnawing at my resolve.

Then Lord Carnahorn spoke, his voice cutting through my doubts like a blade. "I stand with you," he declared. "My resources are at your disposal—my knowledge and my magic."

Relief washed over me like a cleansing tide, leaving behind only gratitude and a sense of unity that bolstered my spirit. I glanced at Beauty; her expression mirrored my own—a mixture of relief and gratitude so profound it needed no words.

"Thank you," I said to Lord Carnahorn, each word infused with the depth of my appreciation. His support was more than just an addition to our strength; it was validation—a beacon in the encroaching darkness.

As we discussed strategies and shared knowledge, I felt the power of unity weaving its magic around us. We were not alone in this fight; we were part of something greater—a collective force bound by honor and driven by a shared purpose.

Lord Carnahorn's willingness to stand with us marked a turning point in our journey—a beacon of hope that reignited the flame within me. With allies like him at our side, we would face whatever challenges lay ahead with renewed vigor and unwavering courage.

In that council room, surrounded by ancient stone and echoes of past deliberations, I realized that together we were more than just two souls bound by destiny—we were leaders forging a future for our people. And as long as we stood united, there was nothing we could not overcome.

Night had descended upon the castle like a cloak, wrapping its stone walls in shadows and silence. I stood upon the battlements, gazing into the vastness that stretched beyond our domain. The air was still, yet it felt charged, as if the very essence of magic hung heavy around us.

The darkness was not complete; the stars were oddly absent from the sky tonight, and that alone was enough to stir unease within me. Then, without warning, the unnatural stillness broke as a dark cloud began to form on the horizon. It swirled and grew at an alarming rate, a malevolent dance of shadows that twisted and writhed against the night sky.

A cold shiver ran down my spine. "This can't be good," I muttered under my breath, my instincts on high alert. The darkness of the cloud seemed to seep into my very bones, a harbinger of ill omens yet to unfold.

As if summoned by my thoughts, a messenger—pale as death itself—rushed to my side. His eyes were wide with fear, his breaths coming in ragged gasps as he struggled to speak. "My lord," he stammered, "there's been a disturbance in the eastern forests. Something... unnatural."

My fists clenched at my sides, nails digging into my palms. The prophecy's challenges—those we had been bracing ourselves for—were no longer distant threats whispered in hushed tones. They were upon us now, as real and as dangerous as the blade of a sword.

"We'll face this together," I affirmed silently to myself, turning back towards the safety of the castle walls. The path ahead would be fraught with peril, but I knew that together we were stronger than any curse or prophecy could ever hope to be.

Gathering my cloak about me to fend off the chill that had nothing to do with the night air, I made my way down from the battlements with purposeful strides. Each step was a promise—a vow that I would stand before whatever darkness came our way and protect what was most precious.

There would be no rest tonight; we had preparations to make, defenses to bolster. And as I walked through the echoing corridors of our ancient home, I knew that no matter what lay ahead, we would meet it head-on with courage and unwavering determination—for our kingdom, for our family, for each other.

Kindled Courage

Beauty

The castle library had become a sanctuary of secrets, its ancient tomes and dust-laden scrolls whispering of times long past. I moved through the labyrinth of knowledge, each step a silent plea for wisdom to aid our quest. Eirian's presence was a steady flame beside me, his focus as unwavering as my own.

I carefully turned the brittle pages of a leather-bound grimoire, its spine crackling in protest. "We need to understand every detail," I murmured, my eyes hungrily scanning the faded script. The words danced before me, a cryptic ballet of history and prophecy intertwined.

"Indeed," Eirian's voice echoed softly in the hush of the room. "The past holds the keys to our future."

My fingers traced the worn pages, my mind racing to connect the dots. The flickering candlelight cast a warm glow upon our work, but inside, I felt a cold urgency clawing at my chest. Every detail matters, I thought, glancing at Eirian who was equally engrossed in a tome of his own. My heart swelled with determination. We can't afford to miss anything.

The air was thick with the musk of old parchment and whispered secrets. I leaned closer to an illuminated manuscript, its pages alive with vibrant colors that belied their age. Here lay an illustration of dragon shifters in their dual forms—majestic and terrifying in equal measure—a visual echo of the very essence we shared.

A chill skittered down my spine as I read aloud, "When the last heir wields the flame of ancients against the shadow's maw, only then shall light rebirth or darkness devour all." The prophecy seemed to stare back at me from the page, its meaning clear yet enigmatic.

Eirian's hand found mine atop the ancient text, grounding me as my thoughts spiraled. "Together," he said firmly, "we will face whatever comes." His touch was both an anchor and a promise—a silent vow that we would not be torn asunder by fates cruel or kind.

With each word we unearthed, the tapestry of our ancestors' legacies grew more intricate. It was a tale woven with threads of power and sacrifice—a narrative that now entwined with our own. In that moment, I knew our journey was more than a quest; it was destiny unfurling beneath our fingertips.

I caught Eirian's eye, and we shared a moment of mutual understanding and resolve. The gravity of our task weighed heavily upon us, but it was our shared mission that fortified my resolve. Together we stood on the precipice of history—guardians of a future yet unwritten—and it was ours to defend.

As my fingers brushed against the spines of the ancient tomes, a peculiar outline drew my attention. Hidden amidst the vast chronicles of our forebears, there it was—a fine seam barely visible in the woodwork of the shelf. My heart fluttered with anticipation; secrets whispered through the ages beckoned me closer. With a soft breath, I pressed against the carved insignia, and to my astonishment, a hidden latch yielded under my touch.

With a gentle click, a compartment no larger than a book itself revealed its presence. The dust of centuries parted as I opened the narrow door to unveil an ancestral journal, its cover embossed with the emblem of my lineage—the intertwining of dragon and shifter in an eternal dance.

"This... this could be the key," I murmured, scarcely believing what lay cradled in my hands. The leather was supple despite its age, and as I opened it, the pages sang with a crackle that resonated in the silent library. The ink had faded but not faltered; every word penned by an ancestor's hand was a fragment of our shared past—a legacy waiting to be understood.

Eirian looked up from his own research, his eyes meeting mine across the room. The flicker of candlelight danced across his features, casting shadows that spoke of mysteries yet unraveled. "What have you found?" he asked, his voice a low thrum that vibrated with curiosity.

"Look at this," I said, my voice trembling with excitement as I crossed the room to where he stood. The journal felt heavy with promise as I laid it before him on the table strewn with maps and manuscripts.

Together we pored over the entries, our heads bowed in shared concentration. There were tales of valor and sorrow, triumphs interlaced with tragedies—all culminating in a revelation that set my pulse racing.

A technique—a secret that had been lost to time—promised an advantage against those who would threaten our realm. It spoke of harnessing the elements in ways I had never imagined; a fusion of dragon fire and shifter spirit that could tip the scales in our favor.

My hands shook as I absorbed the implications. This was more than mere knowledge; it was hope crystallized into words. It was power that had once been wielded by those who shared my blood—a power that now rested on our shoulders to master.

"We must learn this," I said, determination steeling my voice as Eirian and I exchanged a look of fierce resolve. There was no time to waste; our enemies would not rest, and neither could we. The journal was not just a window into our history—it was a beacon guiding us toward victory.

With each page turned, I felt a surge of connection to those who came before us. They had entrusted their wisdom to these pages, and now it was up to Eirian and me to carry their legacy forward.

The air in my study was thick with anticipation, the only sound the crackle of the fire and the rustle of parchment. Eirian and I leaned over the ancient journal, its revelations laid bare under the flickering candlelight. My finger paused over a particularly intricate diagram, tracing the lines that seemed to vibrate with power.

"This changes everything," I breathed, the weight of our discovery anchoring me to the moment. I could see it now—the secret technique of my ancestors, a legacy of fire and spirit woven into one. It was a dance of elements, a confluence of dragon might and shifter finesse that could very well shift the tide in our favor.

Eirian's gaze met mine, his eyes a mirror to my own resolve. "We can integrate this into our defenses, perhaps even use it to enhance our attack," he suggested, his voice steady but I could hear the undercurrent of excitement.

I nodded, my mind already sifting through possibilities. "We'll need to practice, to master this technique until it's second nature." The thought sent a thrill through me. To wield such power... it was both exhilarating and daunting.

Pulling a map closer, I traced routes and marked strategic locations where we could employ our newfound advantage. Eirian's hand hovered over mine, his touch sending a jolt of warmth up my arm. Together, we plotted each move with meticulous care.

"We have what we need to turn the tide," I thought, a surge of optimism blossoming within me. Our close proximity as we bent over the maps created an electric tension, a silent acknowledgment of our unity against the darkness that threatened to engulf our kingdom.

"Training begins at dawn," I said with newfound authority, feeling my confidence swell with each word. "We'll start in the courtyard; it's secluded enough for privacy."

Eirian nodded, his eyes never leaving mine. "I'll be ready," he promised.

As he stood to leave, his hand brushed mine—a fleeting touch that spoke volumes. In that simple gesture lay trust, camaraderie... and something deeper that made my heart flutter against my ribs.

With Eirian's departure, silence once again claimed my study. Yet it was no longer oppressive; it hummed with potential and whispered promises of victory. As I rolled up the maps and tucked away the journal, I knew that sleep would elude me tonight. But it mattered little—for in my veins coursed the fire of dragons and the determination of kings. And come morning, we would rise—together—to face whatever darkness awaited us.

The council room was steeped in antiquity, its walls lined with the wisdom of ages past. Sunlight filtered through stained glass, casting a kaleidoscope of colors that danced upon the faces of the elders seated before us. The air was thick with the scent of incense, each breath I took seemed to fill me with a sense of solemnity.

Eirian stood beside me, his presence a towering pillar of support. We faced the council together, united by our shared burden and the unspoken vows we had made to each other. With a deep breath, I unfolded the prophecy before them, my voice steady despite the tremors that threatened to betray my inner turmoil.

"This prophecy speaks of ancient times," I began, watching as recognition dawned in their age-lined eyes. They listened intently as I recounted our journey thus far, the challenges we had faced, and the enigmatic future that lay shrouded in mystery before us.

An elder with hair like threads of silver leaned forward, his eyes piercing as he spoke. "You must seek allies who understand the old ways," he said, his voice resonating with authority and wisdom born from a lifetime of service to the kingdom. "There are those who still remember, those who hold the keys to forgotten lore."

Another advisor, her face a map of lifelines etched by time and care, added her voice to the chorus. "But be wary," she cautioned. "For enemies lurk in shadows you have yet to cast."

Their words were like stones cast into still waters, ripples of knowledge spreading out to touch distant shores within my mind. Potential allies and enemies—pieces on a board that was larger and more complex than I had ever imagined.

Eirian's hand found mine beneath the table, his grip firm and reassuring. It was a silent message that spoke volumes: we were not alone in this fight.

As we absorbed their guidance, I felt a sense of reassurance washing over me like a gentle tide. These were not just elders; they were guardians of our kingdom's history, keepers of secrets that had been passed down through generations.

"We will heed your counsel," Eirian declared, his voice carrying the weight of his royal lineage. The elders nodded in approval, their expressions grave yet tinged with hope.

I knew then that our path would be fraught with dangers both known and unforeseen. But as Eirian and I stood up to leave the council room, I felt my resolve harden like steel tempered in fire. With each step we took back into the light of day, our determination grew stronger.

We would face whatever lay ahead with courage and unity—for our kingdom's sake, for our love's sake, for the sake of all who depended on us to weave a future from the threads of prophecy and fate.

The clang of metal and the scent of oil filled the air as I entered the castle armory, a place of preparation and resolve. My eyes darted over the rows of gleaming weapons, each one a silent promise to protect our future. Eirian stood at a table, maps and scrolls spread before him, his brow creased in concentration.

"We need to be ready for anything," I said, my voice steady despite the flutter of nerves in my stomach. Eirian looked up, his gaze meeting mine, and in his eyes, I saw a reflection of my own determination.

"I've sent word to the allies we can trust," he replied, rolling up a map with practiced hands. "They will come."

I nodded, comforted by the thought of our friends joining us in this fight. We had been through so much together already—battles fought, secrets uncovered, hearts entwined. This was just another chapter in our story, one we would write with courage.

Together, we walked through the armory. Eirian selected a sword, its blade singing as he drew it from its sheath. I chose a set of lightweight armor that would not hinder my movements when I shifted into my dragon form. Every piece was a part of our arsenal against the unknown trials prophesied to come.

In the study room, surrounded by ancient texts that whispered secrets of a time long past, we poured over strategies and contingencies. The weight of our responsibility was like a mantle upon our shoulders—a mantle we bore with pride.

"We've faced danger before," Eirian said, his hand coming to rest on my shoulder—a touch that spoke volumes of the trust between us.

"And we will face it again," I finished for him. His confidence bolstered my own, chasing away the tendrils of doubt that sought to creep into my heart.

"Together," I affirmed, and it was more than just a word—it was a vow.

The hours slipped by as we worked side by side, each plan sharpened to perfection like the blades that hung on the walls around us. As night fell and stars began to dot the sky outside the window, we knew that we had done all we could to prepare for what lay ahead.

Our path was shrouded in mystery and fraught with peril, but we would meet it head-on. For we were more than just prince and dragon shifter; we were warriors forged in fire and ice, bound by love and destined for greatness. And no prophecy—no matter how dire—could ever change that.

Dawn had barely kissed the horizon when I stepped onto the training grounds, the chill of the morning air biting at my cheeks. Eirian was already there, his silhouette etched against the pale light, a silent testament to his resolve. We had one purpose: to master the ancient technique that could tip the scales in our favor.

I drew my sword, the familiar weight of it grounding me as I centered myself for the day's training. Eirian mirrored my movements, and together we began the intricate dance of shifter and dragon—a melding of forms and power that our ancestors had wielded with devastating effect.

The clang of swords set a rhythm to our movements, punctuating the stillness of the morning with the sound of steel against steel. I moved with precision, each step deliberate, each breath a silent incantation of focus. My muscles protested, but I pushed through the discomfort, sweat beading on my brow as I honed my body to obey my will.

"We need to be perfect," I said to Eirian, my voice steady as a drumbeat. His nod was all the reply I needed; his own determination was a palpable force that spurred me on.

With every passing hour, we drilled under the watchful eyes of dawn. Our movements became more fluid, more assured—two halves of a whole moving in harmony. The ancient technique was more than mere combat; it was an art form that required both dragon fire and shifter grace.

As midday approached, I felt the burn in my limbs, a testament to our relentless pursuit of mastery. But there was no room for fatigue—not when so much was at stake. With each drop of sweat that fell to the earth, I felt a growing sense of readiness take root within me.

Eirian moved with a ferocity that matched my own, his eyes alight with an inner flame that only seemed to grow brighter with each challenge we faced. "Again," he urged after a particularly grueling sequence, and I squared my shoulders in response.

We trained until the sun reached its zenith, until our shadows were mere puddles beneath our feet. And as we paused for respite, our chests heaving in unison from exertion, I knew that we were inching closer to what we needed to be—not just warriors but guardians of a future that teetered on the brink between light and shadow.

Our shared purpose bound us tighter than any chain could—a bond forged in sweat and steel. And as we readied ourselves for another round of training, I knew that together, Eirian and I would face whatever darkness lay ahead. We were ready—we had to be.

As I stepped onto the makeshift dais in the castle courtyard, my heart thundered against my ribcage. A sea of faces turned toward me—stalwart warriors, steadfast servants, and resilient villagers—all united under the banner of our shared cause. Their eyes, brimming with trust and expectation, anchored me to the moment. It was a mantle of leadership I never expected to wear, yet as I gazed upon them, a swell of pride rose within me.

I drew in a deep breath, letting the crisp air fill my lungs and steel my resolve. "My friends," I began, my voice echoing off the stone walls, "we stand on the precipice of a battle that will decide the fate of our kingdom."

A hush fell over the crowd as they hung on my words. I could feel Eirian's presence beside me, a steady force of assurance. I glanced at him briefly, drawing strength from his unwavering support before continuing.

"Each one of you has shown courage beyond measure," I said, sweeping my gaze across the faces before me. "You have stood firm against the shadows that sought to claim our home. And now," I paused, letting my eyes lock with as many as I could, "we must stand together once more."

I stepped forward, the cobblestones cool beneath my boots. "Together, we will face whatever comes," I declared, my voice resonating with a strength that surprised even me. A ripple of affirmation surged through the crowd like a wave cresting against the shore.

Murmurs of agreement swelled into a unified cheer that filled the courtyard and soared beyond its confines. It was more than mere noise; it was the sound of hope igniting, of disparate hearts beating as one.

"We are not alone in this fight," I thought as I let their voices wash over me. The weight of leadership pressed upon my shoulders, yet it was not a burden—it was an honor.

I raised my hand, signaling for silence, and waited until their eager faces returned their attention to me. "Let us go forth with courage in our hearts and steel in our hands," I said with conviction. "For we are dragon kin—unyielding and bound by blood and bravery!"

Their response was immediate—a thunderous applause that seemed to shake the very earth beneath us. Eirian stepped forward then, placing a reassuring hand on my shoulder.

As the echo of their cheers faded into a determined silence, I knew we were ready. For this moment, for this fight—for whatever destiny awaited us beyond the castle walls.

The cool twilight wrapped the garden in a cloak of tranquility, a stark contrast to the cacophony of the day's preparations. Eirian and I found solace on a secluded balcony, our sanctuary from the world's demands. The moon, a silver crescent, hung low in the sky, casting a gentle luminescence over us.

We sat close, our fingers entwined, each touch a silent promise. The air was perfumed with the scent of night-blooming flowers, their petals unfurling in the moon's tender light. It was here, away from prying eyes and ears, that we allowed ourselves to be vulnerable.

"I'm scared," I whispered, the admission escaping my lips before I could rein it in. The words hovered between us like fragile butterflies.

Eirian turned to me, his face softened by shadows and understanding. His thumb brushed over my knuckles in a soothing rhythm. "No matter what happens, we face it together," he said, his voice a low rumble that resonated within my chest.

Our fears and hopes lay bare in that shared silence, intertwining like the vines climbing the balcony's stone railing. His presence was a balm to my frayed nerves; with him beside me, I felt an unwavering strength coursing through my veins.

I leaned into him, resting my head against his shoulder. His warmth enveloped me—a fortress against the chill of doubt. "With you, I can face anything," I thought, allowing myself to draw comfort from his steady heartbeat against my cheek.

The weight of what lay ahead pressed upon us both—dark clouds on the horizon of our destiny—but in this moment of quietude, we found an anchor in each other's embrace. It was a tenderness that fortified our resolve; for together we were more than just Beauty and the Dragon Beast—we were two halves of a whole.

As the night deepened around us, we remained there, cocooned in our shared resolve. The stars above whispered tales of ancient battles and timeless love—a tapestry to which our own story was now woven. And though tomorrow would bring with it the roar of war and the tempest of fate, tonight we basked in the silent symphony of our unity.

The war room's air was thick with anticipation, a living thing that seemed to pulse with the same nervous energy coursing through my veins. The clatter of armor and the low murmur of voices merged into a battle hymn that set my heart racing. I stood at the center of it all, the weight of my destiny pressing down on me like the heavy metal cuirass protecting my chest.

A messenger, cloaked in the urgency of his news, burst through the doors. His eyes found mine across the crowded space, and in that instant, I knew. I strode forward, my hand outstretched for the parchment clutched in his grasp.

"The enemy moves," he panted, his words slicing through the din like a well-honed blade.

I unfurled the message with trembling hands, but my voice was steady as stone when I spoke. "The time has come," I announced, and heads turned toward me, drawn by the resolve in my tone.

Without hesitation, I moved through the war room, touching shoulders and meeting eyes. "To arms!" I called out, and like a spark to tinder, the room ignited into action.

I slipped away to don my armor in solitude. The cold metal kissed my skin as I fastened each piece into place. Eirian entered silently, his own armor a dark mirror of mine. Our eyes met in the dim light, and wordlessly we shared our fears and our determination.

"We're ready," I thought as I clasped my gauntlets tight. The familiar weight settled around me—a comforting embrace that steeled my resolve. "For our kingdom, for our future," I vowed silently.

Eirian nodded once, gravely. "We stand together," he said, his voice low and fierce.

I reached for my sword, feeling its balance and promise in my hand. "Then let us meet them as one," I replied.

Together we stepped into the courtyard where our allies gathered—a sea of faces marked by hope and trepidation. They looked to us, their prince and their dragon shifter heir, for reassurance that we could weather this storm.

As I raised my sword high above me, a beacon in the gathering darkness, a roar rose up from their throats—a roar of courage over fear, unity over division.

The enemy was coming. But we were ready. We were dragon-strong and lion-hearted. And we would protect this kingdom with every last beat of our fiery hearts. Our journey begins.

Forged in Frost and Flame

Beauty

As we stood at the border of the volcanic badlands, the earth beneath our feet felt like the crust of a baked world, fissured and brittle. I squinted against the acrid smoke that hung in the air, a curtain of ash that veiled the sun's fury. The land before us was an artist's canvas of destruction: molten rivers carving paths through charred stone, pits of bubbling lava belching fiery breath, and the sky painted with a palette of angry oranges and sullen reds.

I could feel Eirian's gaze on me, his presence a steady force at my side. I turned to look at him, his dark eyes reflecting the inferno that stretched out before us. His hand found mine, calloused and warm, and I latched onto it as if it were my lifeline amidst this smoldering chaos.

"This place... it's like walking into the maw of a dragon," I murmured, my voice barely rising above the crackle and hiss of the badlands.

Eirian nodded solemnly. "It is unforgiving, but we will traverse it together." His voice was a low rumble, as resolute as the ground we dared to tread upon.

My grip on his hand tightened involuntarily. I could feel sweat beading on my brow, not just from the oppressive heat but from the weight of apprehension that pressed upon my chest. Yet beneath that trepidation was something stronger—a fierce determination that surged through my veins like wildfire.

We took our first steps into this hellish landscape together. With each cautious stride, I felt an odd kinship with this place. It was deadly and volatile, much like the dragon blood that pulsed within me—a reminder of both the power I wielded and the peril that came with it.

"We must be vigilant," Eirian said as we navigated around a steaming fissure. "The ground is treacherous, and these flames are unforgiving."

I nodded in agreement, swallowing down my fear. "We will face whatever comes," I replied with a steadiness I hoped was convincing. "Together."

The heat wrapped around us like a suffocating shroud as we ventured deeper into the badlands. But within me burned something hotter still—the fire of my lineage and an unyielding resolve to overcome whatever trials awaited us in this scorched expanse.

As we moved forward, side by side, our silhouettes cast long shadows behind us—a testament to our unity against the adversities ahead.

We delved deeper into the volcanic badlands, where the air turned thick with sulfur and the ground trembled beneath our feet. Each step was a silent prayer, a plea to the ancient forces slumbering in this forsaken place. The narrow paths wound treacherously between steaming vents and sudden, vicious spurts of lava that seemed to claw at the sky before plunging back into the depths.

Eirian moved with a focus so sharp it could slice through the dense heat that hung around us. "Stay close, Beauty. Watch your step," he cautioned over his shoulder, his voice firm yet laced with an undercurrent of concern that only I could detect.

I trailed behind him, my senses on edge. The crackling of the earth's crust underfoot was a constant reminder of the dangers we faced. With every near miss, my heart thrashed against my ribs, threatening to burst. "We can't afford a single mistake," I whispered to myself, more mantra than observation. I had to be strong—not just for my sake but for Eirian's too.

His back was a constant in my vision—broad and reassuring. The heat from the ground seeped through the soles of my boots, yet it was his presence that kept me grounded. His silhouette against the glow of molten rock was both a beacon and a warning: there was light even in darkness, but also peril.

As we navigated this hellish labyrinth, a geyser erupted mere steps from us, spewing scalding water into the air with a roar that drowned out all thought. Instinctively, I reached for Eirian's arm, pulling him back from the blast. Our eyes met for an electric moment—mine wide with fear, his narrowed in determination—and then he nodded at me, a silent thank you etched in the lines of his face.

We continued on, each step measured and cautious. The paths grew narrower still, forcing us to move in an almost rhythmic synchrony as if we were two halves of one being—dancing on the edge of destruction.

The sulfurous fumes clawed at my throat and eyes, but I kept them open wide, unwilling to miss any sign of impending danger. Eirian's voice cut through the haze once more: "We're almost through." His words were meant to reassure me, but they carried the weight of unsaid prayers—for our safety and for our mission's success.

My gaze never left him as we moved together through this treacherous domain. With every step we took side by side, I felt our bond solidify—a union formed not just by shared goals but by shared peril and unwavering trust.

We stumbled upon the cave by chance, its mouth agape like a silent sentinel offering sanctuary from the inferno outside. Eirian entered first, his tall frame disappearing into the shadows, and I followed, my breath catching at the sudden drop in temperature. The air inside was a balm to my scorched skin, a gentle caress after the relentless assault of the badlands' heat.

The cave's interior was simple and unadorned, save for the faint glow of lava seeping through the cracks, casting eerie shadows on the walls. We settled on the cool stone floor, our backs against the rough wall, and I couldn't help but let out a sigh of relief. For a moment, just a fleeting moment, we were no longer warriors on an arduous quest; we were simply two souls seeking respite.

Eirian handed me a water flask, his fingers brushing against mine. "Drink," he urged softly. "You need it."

I took a grateful sip, feeling the cool liquid slide down my throat. "Thank you," I murmured, handing it back to him. Our eyes met in the dim light, and something unspoken passed between us—a recognition of our shared struggles and an acknowledgment of our growing bond.

"We make a great team," I said with a small smile, breaking the silence that had enveloped us.

He returned my smile with one of his own, rare and heartening. "We're stronger together," he agreed, nodding toward our meager provisions spread between us. "Now let's plan our next steps."

As we discussed our strategy, I found myself admiring his tactical mind, his ability to see paths through chaos. But it was more than that—it was his unwavering support that bolstered me. In this cave, shielded from the outside world's fury, I realized how deeply I had come to rely on him.

I leaned closer to him as we pored over our maps and notes. Our shoulders touched—a simple contact that sent warmth radiating through me. It was strange how such small gestures could forge such profound connections.

"In the morning," Eirian said thoughtfully, tracing a route with his finger, "we'll head north. There's an old bridge marked here—it might be our best chance to cross into less hostile territory."

I nodded in agreement. The thought of leaving this temporary sanctuary was daunting, yet knowing that Eirian would be by my side made all the difference. As we settled down to catch some sleep before dawn's approach, I felt an immense sense of camaraderie enveloping us.

In this quiet cave, with only each other for company, I knew we were more than just allies—we were partners in every sense of the word. And together, we would face whatever lay ahead.

As we left the inferno of the volcanic badlands behind, a frigid gust swept over us, as if to cleanse away the clinging ash and sweat from our perilous trek. The air shifted, growing sharper with each step until it bit at my cheeks with invisible teeth. It was a cold that seeped through my clothing and gnawed at my bones—a harbinger of the icy wasteland that lay before us.

The scorched earth beneath our feet gave way to a crunching carpet of snow. My boots, still warm from the badlands' heat, left steaming impressions that were quickly swallowed by the frost. I shivered, drawing my cloak tighter around me. "It's like stepping into another world," I whispered, more to myself than to Eirian.

His arm came around me in a gesture that was part protective, part supportive. "We need to find shelter soon," he said, his voice carrying an edge of urgency that mirrored the bite of the cold.

I looked up at him, grateful for the warmth of his presence and the solidity of his frame against the chill. Despite the shock of this abrupt transition from fire to ice, I felt a surge of determination pulse through me. This was just another test, another trial on our journey—one we would face as we had all others: together.

The landscape stretched before us in rolling hills and valleys, all blanketed in a thick layer of snow that glimmered under the wan light of a half-moon. In the distance, jagged mountains loomed like silent giants, their peaks veiled by clouds and mystery.

As we trudged onward, Eirian's grip on me never wavered. His protective nature was a comfort in this desolate place where every shadow could conceal a threat. "We'll need to keep our wits about us," he said, scanning the horizon. "The ice can be as treacherous as any fire."

I nodded, feeling his words resonate within me. We were out of one danger and into another—such was our path, fraught with peril at every turn. But within me burned a fire no winter could quench: the fire of my dragon blood.

With Eirian by my side and the legacy of my ancestors within me, I felt ready to face whatever lay ahead in this icy domain. We moved forward together into the heart of winter's domain, braced against its cold embrace but never yielding to it.

The icy wasteland stretched before us, a merciless expanse of white that blurred the line between earth and sky. With each step, the snow's crunch was a stark reminder of the frozen desert's desolation. The wind howled like a pack of ravenous wolves, its biting chill gnawing through my cloak and sinking its teeth into my flesh. I pulled the fabric tighter around me, but it was no match for the cold that seemed intent on claiming us.

"We can't give up now," I murmured to myself, my breath forming a ghostly cloud in the frigid air. My words were snatched away by the wind, yet they bolstered my resolve. Beside me, Eirian's presence was a beacon of strength; his towering form cut through the storm like a steadfast ship navigating turbulent seas.

His eyes met mine, reflecting the ice-swept landscape and a glimmer of concern. "We're close, just a bit further," he said, his voice barely audible over the storm's roar. But his reassurance was more than words—it was a lifeline in this frozen abyss.

I nodded, though every fiber of my being screamed for shelter, for warmth—for an end to this relentless assault. Yet surrender was not an option; not when we had come so far, not when our kingdom's fate hung in the balance. So we pressed on, our bodies hunched against the wind's wrath, our steps synchronized in silent determination.

Eirian reached out, his gloved hand finding mine, and interlaced our fingers. The gesture was simple but filled with unspoken promises—of protection, of shared burdens. His grip was firm and warm despite the cold that sought to leech away our very lifeblood.

The storm intensified, its icy breath a sharp contrast to the volcanic heat we had left behind. Snowflakes lashed against my face like tiny shards of glass, each one a reminder of Freya's lingering malice. This wasteland was her doing—a kingdom encased in her frosty spite.

Yet as I trudged forward, leaning into Eirian's side for support, I realized that even in this barren place there was beauty. The way ice crystals danced in the tempest's fury; how each snowflake held within it an intricate pattern—a unique testament to nature's resilience.

I allowed myself to draw strength from these observations, to find wonder amidst adversity. It was this perspective—this refusal to be cowed by hardship—that had carried me through every trial thus far.

As we moved through the blizzard's heart, I knew that whatever lay ahead would test us further. But together—with Eirian by my side—I felt invincible against even the coldest winter's embrace.

We trudged through the endless white, my mind numb from the biting cold and my body weary. Yet, when we stumbled upon a small clearing shielded by a ring of frosted trees, something stirred within me—a flicker of hope that refused to be smothered by the icy desolation.

In the center of the clearing stood a solitary rock, its surface adorned with ancient markings. I approached it, drawn by an inexplicable pull. "Eirian, look," I called out, my voice barely above a whisper as I traced the symbols with my fingers.

The etchings were old, weathered by time and the harsh elements, but unmistakably deliberate. Depictions of dragons intertwined with elements—flames, waves, gusts of wind, and what appeared to be shards of ice—formed a circular pattern around the rock's perimeter.

"This is a sign," I murmured to myself, the realization dawning on me like the first rays of dawn piercing through a long night. My heart quickened as I circled the rock, each symbol igniting a sense of purpose in my chest.

Eirian joined me, his gaze intense as he studied the markings. "We're not alone in this," he said firmly. The determination in his voice bolstered my own, grounding me in the present and the mission at hand.

He was right. These symbols were left here for us—for me. They were guidance from my ancestors, a breadcrumb trail leading us through Freya's icy labyrinth to her fortress.

My eyes roamed over the etchings once more before settling on an image that seemed to stand out—a dragon with its wings unfurled in flight and its maw open in what looked like a roar or perhaps... a call. Beneath it was a series of lines and curves that resembled a rudimentary map.

"This way," I said with conviction, pointing towards the north where the lines led. My voice was stronger now, infused with an energy that defied the cold that sought to claim us.

The discovery reignited our determination like dry tinder kissed by flame. With renewed vigor, we followed where the ancient markings beckoned us. Each step felt surer than the last; each breath less burdened.

As we left the clearing behind us, stepping back into the expanse of snow and ice that stretched toward our unknown future, I knew we had found our path forward. And for the first time since embarking on this perilous journey, I allowed myself to truly believe that we would succeed.

The wind outside our makeshift shelter howled like a beast in agony, yet within the circle of warmth from our small fire, it seemed a world away. Eirian and I sat close, the flames casting dancing shadows upon his features, softening the hard lines of worry that had etched themselves into his face during our journey.

He reached out, his hand finding mine in the dim light, and I felt a current pass between us—an unspoken understanding that we were bound together by more than just our quest. His fingers were warm and sure, their strength a contrast to the gentle way he caressed my palm.

"We've come so far together," I said, my voice barely above a whisper. Memories of our trials flickered through my mind like the fire before us—every challenge faced, every fear overcome. "And we will see this through to the end."

Eirian's gaze met mine, his eyes reflecting the firelight and something deeper, something that stirred within my chest—a fierce tenderness that I had only ever felt in his presence. "We will succeed because we're together," he replied with a soft certainty that wrapped around me like a blanket.

I nodded, feeling the weight of his words settle in my heart. There was truth in them—a truth as clear and bright as the flame that separated us from the frozen darkness. In his eyes, I saw not only the prince who had endured so much pain but also the man who had grown alongside me, who had shared in my laughter and my tears.

The wind rose in pitch outside our shelter, a reminder of the harsh world waiting beyond our haven of warmth. But within this moment, within this small space carved out of ice and desolation, there was only us—two souls intertwined by fate and choice.

"Our bond has been forged in fire and tested in ice," I said, squeezing his hand. "And it will not break."

Eirian leaned closer, his breath warm against my cheek as he whispered, "Together we are stronger than any curse."

I closed my eyes for a moment, allowing myself to fully feel the depth of our connection—the way it had grown from cautious alliance to something profound and unshakeable. When I opened them again, Eirian was watching me with an intensity that made my heart quicken.

In that quiet space filled with shared warmth and whispered vows, I knew that no matter what lay ahead for us in the icy expanse beyond our shelter's walls, we would face it together—with courage in our hearts and an unwavering belief in each other.

Dragonfire's Defiance

Prince Eirian

The air was sharp with the tang of ice and the scent of storm-brewed ozone as we approached the fortress. It stood like a monolith against the roiling clouds, a stark silhouette etched with malice and the cold whispers of forgotten sorrows. Beauty's scales glinted beside me, reflecting the fitful light that broke through the cloud cover, her form a testament to the resilience and courage that had brought us to this precipice of destiny.

"This is it," I murmured, my voice a rumble deep within my chest. The weight of our journey, every trial we had faced together, bore down on me with an almost physical pressure. "We've come too far to fail now."

Beauty shifted slightly, her dragon form shimmering as she briefly returned to her human guise. She reached out, her hand finding mine with unerring precision. "We'll face this together," she said, her voice steady as the rock beneath our feet. Her eyes were pools of molten gold, alight with a fierce determination that matched my own.

I squeezed her hand, feeling the warmth of her skin against my scales. It was a lifeline, a reminder that I was no longer alone in my cursed existence. We had forged something unbreakable, something that went beyond the bounds of magic and into the very essence of who we were.

As we neared the gates, every instinct screamed at me to turn back, to flee from what awaited us within those walls. But it was that same instinct that drove me forward—the need to protect, to fight for what was right. The curse that had been my torment now served as my armor, my strength bolstered by Beauty's unwavering presence at my side.

The gates loomed before us, dark and foreboding, etched with runes that spoke of ancient magic and darker secrets. I could feel Freya's presence within, a miasma of power and malice that clawed at my senses.

Beauty let go of my hand and transformed once more into her dragon form—a creature of beauty and power that took my breath away every time I beheld her. Together we stood before Freya's fortress, two dragons against the darkness, our hearts beating as one.

"We have to succeed," Beauty whispered on a breath that sent ripples through the frigid air. "For our kingdom. For us."

I nodded, unable to speak past the knot of emotions in my throat. There was no turning back now. We were here to end Freya's reign—to break the chains of fear and winter she had cast upon our land.

And so we stepped forward into shadow and uncertainty, ready to face whatever horrors lay beyond those gates. For love. For redemption. For hope reborn from ashes and ice.

The icy wind howled like a banshee's wail as we stood at the threshold of Freya's fortress. Its walls, dark and foreboding, rose up to meet the tumultuous sky—a barrier between us and the heart of winter's curse. My scales bristled with the chill, but it was not the cold that set my nerves alight—it was the anticipation of battle, the knowledge that within those walls lurked creatures borne of darkness and malice.

I turned to Beauty, her own dragon form a contrast against the stark landscape. Her scales, iridescent with a pale fire, seemed to capture the scant light and refract it into hope. "Stay close," I urged her, my voice a low rumble that danced on the edge of human speech.

"We'll carve our path together," she replied, her voice as steely as her resolve.

As we breached the entrance, Freya's minions descended upon us—a horde of shadows and frost. They came at us with claw and spell, their eyes hollow pits of despair. But they were no match for our fury, for our fire and ice. With every beat of my wings, I unleashed a torrent of flame, scorching those who dared to advance. I shifted between forms with practiced ease, my human cunning guiding my dragon's wrath.

"I won't let them touch her," I vowed silently as Beauty fought beside me. She was magnificent—her power unleashed in chilling waves that froze our enemies in their tracks. The sight filled me with a sense of pride that burned hotter than any flame.

We moved as one—her ice and my fire intertwined in a deadly dance that left no room for mercy. With every enemy that fell, I could feel the weight of years—the burden of my curse—lift ever so slightly. This was what I had been born to do; not to rule from a throne of isolation but to fight for those I had sworn to protect.

As we fought our way through the outer corridors, I could feel Beauty's presence like a beacon in the darkness. She was my anchor in this storm of chaos—a reminder that together we were stronger than any curse or queen.

"We make an unstoppable team," she said, catching my eye amidst the fray.

And she was right. Together there was nothing we could not overcome—no evil we could not vanquish. With every step we took into the heart of Freya's fortress, I knew this truth more profoundly than ever before: united by love and purpose, we were invincible.

The throne room was a cavern of shadows, its walls steeped in dark energy that pulsed like a living thing. Freya sat upon her throne, a queen of ice and malice, her gaze fixed upon us as we entered. Her smile was a razor's edge, cutting through the tension that hung heavy in the air.

I stepped forward, my dragon scales catching the dim light, casting a prismatic glow around us. "This ends now," I declared, my voice reverberating through the vast chamber. The words felt like shackles breaking, the culmination of years of anguish and fury poised to be unleashed.

Within me, fear warred with anger—a tempest that threatened to consume my resolve. I could not falter now, not when Beauty stood beside me, her presence a bastion against the darkness that sought to drown us.

Beauty's dragon eyes gleamed with a fire that no frost could quench. "Together, we can do this," she said, her voice ringing clear and true. I felt the resonance of her conviction bolster my own. She was more than my ally; she was the very heart of my courage.

Freya rose from her throne, her movements languid yet filled with an ominous grace. The shadows seemed to bend to her will, coiling around her like serpents ready to strike. "Seems I have heard those words from you before. You think you can defy me?" she asked, her voice cold as the winds that howled outside her fortress.

I met her gaze squarely, pushing back against the wave of fear that crashed over me. "I don't think—I know," I countered, my stance firm. The power within me surged to life, a flame kindled by years of suffering and stoked by the love I held for Beauty.

"We can't let her win. Not when we're so close," I thought to myself, gripping the hilt of my sword with a determination that left no room for doubt.

Beauty shifted slightly, drawing on the strength of our bond—a connection forged in fire and tempered in ice. "Freya will not break us," she whispered fiercely.

The queen's laughter echoed through the throne room, a sound devoid of warmth or mirth. "Let us see if your resolve is as strong as your words," she taunted.

I squared my shoulders, readying myself for what was to come. Beside me, Beauty did the same, our spirits intertwined and unyielding.

We were two against one, but in this moment, we were an army unto ourselves—a force united by love and driven by a shared purpose: to end Freya's reign and restore warmth to our kingdom's frozen heart.

The throne room erupted into chaos as we faced Freya, the very embodiment of winter's wrath. Her dark magic surged like a tempest, shadows writhing at her command, seeking to entwine us in their icy grasp. Each explosion of her power sent shockwaves through the stone, a relentless assault that threatened to overwhelm us.

But we stood our ground.

I shifted, my dragon form taking precedence as I let out a roar that shook the foundations of the cursed fortress. Scales armored my body against the biting cold, against the onslaught of dark sorcery that Freya hurled with vindictive precision. My claws raked through the air, parrying bolts of ice and shadow that sought to pierce my heart.

"We can't let her win," I thought, my mind racing with tactics even as my muscles ached from exertion. I felt Beauty's presence beside me, her strength flowing into mine. Her icy breath countered Freya's attacks with equal ferocity, a symphony of frost that danced around us, protective and relentless.

The throne room, once a bastion of regal majesty, had transformed into a battleground of cataclysmic fury. Freya stood before us, her silhouette a cold blaze against the darkened hall. My claws dug into the stone, my dragon form unleashed in all its terrifying splendor. Beside me, Beauty's presence was a beacon of fierce determination. We were the last stand against an encroaching abyss.

"We can't let her win," I thought, feeling the heat of my fiery breath billowing in my chest. It erupted from me in a torrential blaze, meeting Freya's shadowy tendrils head-on. Sparks of magic exploded upon impact, casting eerie shadows that danced like mad specters on the walls.

Her laughter pierced the cacophony—a sound as sharp as the icicles that hung from her throne. "You believe love will save you?" Freya taunted, her voice a venomous hiss that slithered through the air.

I roared in defiance, the sound reverberating off the high ceilings and returning to me like an echo of my own rage. Beauty fought with an elegance that belied the ferocity of her attacks, her dragon shifter magic weaving seamlessly with mine. Our powers intertwined—a symphony of ice and fire that held back the night.

"We are one," I realized, feeling our strength surge as one force against Freya's relentless onslaught. Her spells were a tempest, but together we were an immovable force—a bulwark against her storm.

Each strike I delivered was more than just an act of war; it was an affirmation of everything we stood for—of every promise made in whispered confidences and every hope shared under starlit skies. This was our moment to reclaim not just our kingdom but our future.

Freya advanced, her power unfurling like a dark wave set to drown us in despair. Yet we stood unbroken, our unity an unyielding fortress amidst chaos.

"Together, we can defeat her," I vowed silently to Beauty. She nodded, her eyes reflecting a resolve as fierce as the flames we wielded. We were two halves of a whole—her ice to my fire—and nothing would rend us asunder.

With each clash of power, each parry and thrust, I felt the tide turning. Our bond was more than just shared strength; it was a testament to what could be achieved when two souls fought as one.

And so we battled—dragon and dragoness against queen—our love a weapon no dark magic could extinguish.

The throne room was a tempest of ruin, the aftermath of our clash with Freya. My dragon's breath still hung heavy in the air, mixing with the icy remnants of her wrath. We had stood, side by side, a force of nature against the unnatural. And we had nearly triumphed.

But as our victory seemed within grasp, her eyes ignited with an ominous spark. "This is not the end," Freya hissed, her voice a serpentine whisper that seemed to slither through the chaos. And then she was gone—vanished into the ether, leaving behind nothing but a trail of dark mist and the echo of her vow.

I clenched my fists, the frustration boiling within me like molten rock beneath a dormant volcano. "Damn it," I growled under my breath. We had her cornered, and yet she slipped through our fingers like shadows at dusk. The room fell silent but for the crackling remnants of our powers dissipating into nothingness.

Beauty's hand found mine, her touch a balm to the seething anger and helplessness that threatened to consume me. Her fingers interlaced with mine, grounding me back to reality—the reality that Freya was still out there, and we were left to pick up the pieces of her fury.

"What will she do next?" I pondered aloud, my voice barely above a whisper as I surveyed the scorched stone and ice-covered walls that bore witness to our battle. The uncertainty hung over us like a shroud, an unseen adversary in itself.

Beauty's gaze met mine—steadfast and unwavering. "We will find her," I promised, though I knew it was as much a vow to myself as it was to her. Our eyes locked in silent agreement; this fight was far from over.

We stood amid the wreckage of what should have been our triumph—Freya's throne room now nothing more than a mausoleum of her malice. The calm was deceptive; an uneasy lull in a storm we knew had yet to unleash its full fury.

"This isn't over," I said quietly, squeezing Beauty's hand as if to draw strength from her unspoken courage. "Whatever comes next, we'll face it together." And though my voice held determination, inwardly I wrestled with the weight of what lay ahead—the prophecy that loomed over us like an impending eclipse.

For now, we had survived—but survival was merely the first step on a path fraught with peril. For our family, for our kingdom... for everything we held dear... I vowed to stand against whatever darkness awaited us on the horizon.

As Beauty and I stood there, surrounded by silence and the ghostly whispers of battles past and yet to come, one thing remained clear: our resolve would not falter. We would find Freya—and when we did, we would be ready.

Prophecy's Dawn

Beauty

I knelt beside Eirian, the once grand throne room of Freya now a testament to our fierce struggle. Shattered ice and splintered wood littered the floor, a stark contrast to the somber silence that had fallen. My hands, illuminated with a gentle golden glow, hovered above his battered form. The magic that pulsed within me felt warm, almost like a soothing balm as it sought out the shadows of his wounds.

"We did it. We're safe for now," I whispered, my voice barely rising above the quiet. With each word, I poured more of my essence into the healing spell, watching as the cuts and bruises that marred his skin began to fade. Relief washed over me in waves; the terror of possibly losing him ebbed away with each passing second.

Eirian's eyes met mine with a grateful gaze. He winced as he shifted, trying to find a more comfortable position among the debris that surrounded us. His hand found mine, his grip filled with an unspoken promise of gratitude and something deeper, something forged in the crucible of our shared trials.

"Thank you, my love," he murmured, each word laden with weariness and warmth. The connection between us felt tangible, a bond not even Freya's darkest spells could sever.

As I continued to heal him, I couldn't help but reflect on how far we'd come—two souls brought together by fate's cruel twist, now bound by a love that felt as ancient as the magic coursing through our veins. This wasn't just about breaking curses or defeating tyrants; it was about finding our place in a world that seemed determined to keep us apart.

My focus never wavered from Eirian as his injuries healed, but my mind raced ahead—what did this mean for us now? With Freya's threat still looming over us like a storm cloud on the horizon, could we dare to hope for peace? Or was this just the eye of the tempest?

But those thoughts were for another time. For now, in this moment of quiet respite, all that mattered was the man before me and the undeniable truth that together we were stronger than we had ever been apart.

The golden light from my hands began to dim as Eirian's wounds closed completely, leaving no trace of the battle that had raged just moments before. I allowed myself one last glance at his now peaceful expression before pulling back my magic and preparing for whatever lay ahead.

As Eirian rested, his breathing steady and even after the healing, I couldn't resist the pull of curiosity that beckoned me towards the towering bookshelves lining the walls of Freya's throne room. My fingers brushed against the spines of dusty tomes and ancient scrolls, each one a silent guardian of secrets long forgotten. A faint glow caught my eye, a luminescence that seemed to dance between the lines of an old leather-bound book nestled in a shadowed alcove.

With careful hands, I eased the book from its resting place, feeling the weight of centuries in my grasp. The cover was adorned with mystical symbols that resonated with the amulet still warm against my skin. "These might hold the answers we need," I whispered to myself, my heart quickening with each turned page. Eirian's eyes met mine, a silent question within their depths.

"Help me with this," I urged, motioning towards a large scroll sealed with wax that bore the emblem of a dragon entwined with our family crests. Together, we broke the seal and unfurled the parchment on a nearby table cleared of debris.

The script was elegant, flowing like rivers of ink across the paper. Each symbol and drawing pulsed with an energy that seemed familiar yet otherworldly—depictions of dragons and figures robed in regal attire, engaged in rituals and battles that spanned the ages. "Our past and future are intertwined with these words," I realized aloud, tracing a line that connected two figures at the heart of the scroll.

Eirian leaned closer, his interest evident as he studied the images alongside me. "These texts could change everything," he murmured, his voice tinged with awe. His hand hovered over a section that detailed an ancient pact between dragons and humans—a union of strength and wisdom.

"What secrets do these hold?" Eirian mused, his gaze locked on a passage describing a prophecy yet to be fulfilled. The weight of our discovery settled over us like a cloak, heavy with implication and promise.

I could feel it—the stirring of destiny within these brittle pages. It was as if we had stumbled upon a map to our very souls, charting a course through time and legend that led to this very moment. The air around us seemed charged with anticipation as we delved deeper into the texts.

Our quest was far from over; it was evolving, growing into something far greater than either of us could have imagined. With each revelation, our purpose became clearer, our resolve stronger. This was more than just history—it was our legacy, waiting for us to claim it. And as I stood there beside Eirian, surrounded by whispers of the past and echoes of what was yet to come, I knew we were ready to face whatever lay ahead—together.

As I stood in the hushed expanse of Freya's throne room, the silence was a stark contrast to the chaos that had reigned mere hours before. Eirian and I huddled together over a heavy oak table, strewn with the ancient texts we had found concealed within the room's secret alcoves. My fingers traced the intricate diagrams and faded script of a large parchment, the edges curling like autumn leaves.

"This prophecy," I murmured, my voice barely more than a whisper, "it explains so much about our powers and our destiny." A sense of awe washed over me as I connected the symbols before us with the legends I had grown up hearing as bedtime stories. Here they were, not just tales to inspire children to dream, but tangible truths that bound Eirian and me to an ancient lineage.

Eirian leaned closer, his eyes scanning the texts with an intensity that mirrored my own. "We have a great responsibility," he said, his voice a low rumble that resonated through the now-still air. The weight of his gaze met mine, and in that moment, I felt our bond strengthen—a fusion of trust and shared purpose.

"Together," he continued, his hand finding mine across the scattered scrolls, "we can fulfill this prophecy." His touch was firm, grounding me as my mind raced with possibilities and plans.

I nodded, squeezing his hand in return. "We are the key to breaking the curse," I declared, feeling the gravity of our mission settle upon my shoulders like a mantle. The room seemed to echo back my words—a vow made amidst the remnants of a battle hard-won.

Our eyes met again, and I saw in Eirian's gaze not just determination but a reflection of my own resolve. We were two halves of a whole, bound by fate and choice to see this journey through to its end—whatever that may be.

The prophecy spoke of trials and tribulations, of a dragon heir who would rise to either bring unparalleled prosperity or devastating destruction. It was clear that our actions would tip the scales; every choice we made from here on out held the potential to shape the future of our kingdom.

I felt Eirian's grip tighten around my hand—a silent promise that we would face whatever came our way together. And with that unspoken pledge between us, we turned our attention back to the texts. There was much to learn and even more to do. But for now, we had each other and the knowledge that our united strength was far greater than any curse that sought to tear us apart.

In the quiet aftermath, the soft light filtering through the shattered windows of Freya's throne room bathed everything in a serene glow. It was a stark contrast to the chaos that had just unfolded, and as I stood there, taking in the stillness, I felt Eirian's presence beside me like a steadfast beacon.

My gaze found his, and in that moment of reflection, something profound resonated within me. It was as if all the pieces of our journey—each challenge and every shared glance—had led to this realization: our bond was more than just companionship; it was the key to defeating Freya and breaking the curse that had held us in its grip.

"Our love gives us strength," I thought, my heart swelling with an emotion so potent it threatened to overwhelm me. It was an anchor in the stormy seas we had navigated together, a light in the darkness that had threatened to consume us.

I reached out to touch Eirian's face, tracing the line of his jaw with a tenderness that felt as natural as breathing. His skin was warm under my fingertips, a silent testament to the life we fought so fiercely to protect. "With you, we can overcome anything," I whispered, my voice barely audible above the hush.

Eirian's smile was like dawn breaking after a long night. He took my hand in his, and I marveled at how right it felt—the fit of our fingers, the strength in his grip. "Our bond is our greatest weapon," he said, his voice rich with emotion and conviction.

I nodded, feeling an unshakeable determination settle over me. We had faced insurmountable odds, walked through fire and ice together, and emerged not just unscathed but stronger for it. Our love was forged in adversity, tempered by trust and mutual respect. It was a force that even Freya's dark magic could not reckon with.

As we stood amid the ruins of her throne room—a symbol of her shattered ambitions—I knew without a doubt that whatever lay ahead, we would face it together. And with each other by our side, there was nothing we could not conquer.

I knelt on the cold, stone floor of Freya's throne room, carefully rolling up the ancient scrolls that had survived the fury of our confrontation. Each scroll was a treasure trove of our history, a piece of the puzzle that was my heritage and Eirian's curse. "This is just the beginning," I murmured to myself, tucking them into my pack with reverence.

The room was filled with the aftermath of battle, yet within its ravaged walls, I felt a profound sense of relief. We had won, not just against Freya's minions but against the doubts that had plagued us. With each text secured in my bag, my anticipation for the future grew. There was so much to learn, so much to do to ensure our kingdom's safety. "We have so much to do," I said aloud, glancing over at Eirian.

He stood tall and resolute amidst the debris, his wounds already healing thanks to his dragon shifter resilience. His gaze met mine, a silent communication passing between us. He had stood by me through every trial, his strength bolstering my own when I faltered.

"We made it through," he said, echoing my thoughts. His voice was steady, a testament to his regained sense of purpose.

I nodded, my eyes taking in the once-imposing throne room that now stood empty and broken—a symbol of Freya's defeat and our triumph. "Our journey continues," I replied, feeling the truth of those words resonate deep within me.

Eirian approached and helped me to my feet. His touch was gentle yet firm, a reminder of the bond we shared. "Together," he said simply, and I knew he meant more than just leaving this place. Together we would face whatever came next.

As we prepared to leave the fortress that had been both our battleground and a place of revelations, I took one last look around. The throne room was a part of our story now, etched into the fabric of who we were and who we would become.

With Eirian at my side and the weight of our legacy on our shoulders, we stepped through the threshold and into the light beyond Freya's dark domain. We were going home—to heal, to plan, and to build a future where love and determination were our guiding stars.

Triumphant Unity

Prince Eirian

As I strode through the grand halls of the castle, the clamor of preparation was like music, each note a promise of the joy to come. Servants bustled about with floral arrangements, their vibrant colors a stark contrast to the stone walls that had once echoed with my loneliness. Musicians nestled in alcoves, their fingers dancing over strings and woodwinds, tuning the instruments until each chord resonated perfectly in the air.

"This day needs to be flawless," I murmured to myself, feeling the weight of responsibility settle on my shoulders—a weight far lighter than the curse I had borne for so long. Excitement fluttered within me, like a captive bird now free to soar into an endless sky. Today, I would marry Beauty, my heart's true companion on a journey fraught with darkness and light.

I adjusted a candelabrum here, straightened a tapestry there, my eyes scanning every inch of the space that would soon witness our union. The scent of lilies and roses filled my nostrils, a fragrant testament to the life that thrived despite winter's chill grasp finally being broken. "We deserve this moment of happiness," I thought, allowing myself a rare smile as I envisioned our future together—no longer as prince and maiden but as equals in love and power.

The throne room doors stood open, revealing rows of chairs adorned with silken ribbons that fluttered gently in the breeze from the open windows. Sunlight poured through the stained glass, casting kaleidoscopic patterns upon the stone floor—a mosaic of light that seemed to bless the day ahead.

My gaze lingered on the aisle that Beauty would soon walk down, my heart swelling with a love so profound it threatened to overwhelm me. I imagined her there, radiant and strong, her eyes meeting mine with unspoken promises that needed no words to be understood.

I checked over the arrangements one final time, ensuring every detail was a reflection of our journey and our love—a story woven from threads of bravery and sacrifice, now culminating in a tapestry of shared triumph. Each bloom placed with care, each note of music chosen with intention; all of it a testament to what we had overcome together.

Yes, today would be perfect—not because every petal was in place or every candle lit just so, but because it was ours. This celebration was not just a joining of two souls but a declaration to all: love prevails. Love transforms. And above all, love endures.

As the castle courtyard filled with the sound of hooves and the murmur of excited voices, I stood at the entrance, my heart thrumming with a cadence of anticipation. Each arriving guest brought with them a piece of the kingdom, a testament to the land that had weathered the storm of curses and now basked in the promise of renewal.

I welcomed dignitaries with a firm handshake, their formal bows met with a warmth that I hoped conveyed my genuine gratitude. "Thank you for coming," I said, my voice steady and clear. Each face that passed before me was a mirror to our shared history—a tapestry of tales woven from struggle and triumph.

"Our people have come together for this celebration," I thought as I watched a young family approach, their children's eyes wide with wonder. A surge of pride swelled within me as I saw the diversity of our guests—the farmers from the valleys, scholars from the citadels, and artisans from the bustling market towns. All corners of our kingdom were represented here today in a mosaic of unity.

"This wedding symbolizes our unity and strength," I mused silently, my gaze sweeping over the sea of faces. Here was the embodiment of our collective resilience—a people once divided by fear now joined in hope. Each handshake, each smile exchanged, served to fortify my resolve to lead alongside Beauty, to be a prince worthy of such loyalty and courage.

As I greeted an elderly couple who had journeyed far to witness our union, their wrinkled hands clasped tightly together, they offered me a small bundle wrapped in silk. "For you and your bride," they said, their voices harmonizing with years of shared life. "May it bring you joy as you have brought us."

I accepted their gift with a bow of my head, touched by the simplicity and sincerity that marked this offering. It was not just an object within that delicate fabric but a symbol—a beacon of goodwill from those who had seen kingdoms rise and fall.

The courtyard buzzed with laughter and conversation as more guests arrived, each one contributing to the festive atmosphere that seemed to envelop us all. I found myself smiling more freely than I had in years; each expression of joy around me kindled my own happiness.

Indeed, this day was not merely about Beauty and me; it was about all who had stood by us, who had dared to dream of peace and prosperity after enduring the longest winter. As I turned to greet another group of arrivals, I knew that our wedding would be remembered not just as a union between two souls but as a covenant between ruler and realm—a vow to cherish and protect this newfound harmony for all our days.

The grand hall was aglow with a thousand candles, their flames dancing to the tune of the minstrels' song. Laughter and the clinking of goblets filled the air as the guests reveled in the festivities. I stood at Beauty's side, her hand in mine, our fingers entwined like the destinies we were about to join. The warmth of her touch was a balm against any lingering fears that skulked in the shadowed corners of my mind.

It was then that a chill slithered through the jubilant warmth, a harbinger of discord. A figure emerged from the throng, cloaked in shadows that seemed untouched by the merriment around us. Their gait was slow, deliberate, as if each step were measured against the beat of an unseen heart.

"Who would dare threaten us today?" I thought, feeling a surge of protectiveness ripple through me. My eyes narrowed as I faced this unwelcome guest, my grip on Beauty's hand tightening ever so slightly—a silent vow to shield her from any storm.

The figure halted before us, their hooded visage shrouded in mystery. A voice, soft yet laden with menace, slithered from beneath the dark fabric. "Beware the power you seek to control," they whispered. "Not all will celebrate your union."

My heart pounded against my chest, a drumbeat echoing the gravity of their words. I scanned the room quickly; my subjects were oblivious to this veiled threat, lost in their revelry. This confrontation needed to end swiftly, without alarming them.

"We welcome all who come with open hearts," I replied evenly, my voice steady despite the coiled tension within me. "Those who harbor ill will shall find no purchase here."

The figure lingered for a moment longer before melding back into the crowd, disappearing as though they were naught but a specter conjured by doubt. I watched them go, my mind racing with possible dangers and enemies that lurked beyond our sight.

"We will not let fear ruin our day," I resolved inwardly. This was our moment—a celebration of love hard-won and peace restored. Whatever darkness this stranger portended would be faced head-on when the time came.

For now, I turned to Beauty, offering her a reassuring smile that held an unspoken promise: together, we would weather any storm. Her eyes met mine, a mirror to my resolve; they held no trace of fear—only an unwavering trust that fortified my soul.

And so we stood united before our people—undaunted and resolute—as we prepared to step into our future as one.

I felt the whisper of shadows beckoning me as I followed the mysterious guest through the throngs of celebrants. They slipped through the crowd like a wraith, their cloak a mere wisp against the revelry's vibrant tapestry. My heart pounded with a mixture of determination and anger; I needed to know who they were, what dark intentions they harbored on a day that was meant to be filled with nothing but light.

The guest turned down a secluded corridor, one that echoed with the solitude of my former cursed existence. It was here that I quickened my pace, my boots silent upon the stone floor. "I need to know who they are and what they want," I thought, the urgency of my mission sharpening my senses.

I rounded the corner just in time to see the hem of their cloak disappearing around another bend. "Stop!" I commanded, my voice a low growl that seemed to shake the very walls around us. But they did not heed my call; instead, they hastened their retreat.

Finally, I caught up to them, my hand closing around their arm with an iron grip. The corridor seemed to close in on us, the flickering torchlight casting long shadows that played upon our standoff.

"You cannot escape the darkness that follows you," the guest hissed, their voice sharp like the edge of a blade.

I leaned in closer, anger flaring within me as their face remained hidden beneath the hood. "What darkness?" I demanded, my words tinged with both threat and confusion. This day was meant to be a reprieve from shadows and sorrow—a celebration of triumph over curses long past.

For a moment, it seemed as if they might yield, as if the secrets swirling in those shadowed depths would pour forth and reveal themselves to me. But then, with a deftness that betrayed an otherworldly agility, they slipped from my grasp and vanished into the darkness from whence they came.

My fists clenched at my sides as I stared into the empty space where they had stood. "I will protect my family and kingdom," I vowed silently, a promise etched into every fiber of my being. The words of the stranger echoed in my mind—a chilling portent that refused to be ignored.

As I turned back toward the celebration, I felt a resolve settle over me like armor. Whatever this new threat may be, whatever darkness sought to encroach upon our hard-won peace—I would stand ready. And nothing would harm those I held dear; not while I had breath in my body and fire in my soul.

The moon hung like a silver pendant in the velvet sky, casting a serene glow over the castle gardens where Beauty and I had sought refuge from the celebrations. The music and laughter from the grand hall were but a distant echo here, replaced by the soft whisper of the night breeze and the rustle of leaves. In this secluded sanctuary, we found a moment of peace amidst the turmoil that had shaken our day.

Beauty stood beside me, her eyes reflecting the garden's ethereal light. Yet within their depths, I could see the shadow of worry that had crept into her heart since the veiled threat had been uttered. I reached out, my hand gently cupping her cheek, guiding her gaze to meet mine.

"I won't let anything happen to you," I whispered, my voice a low rumble of reassurance. I felt her lean into my touch, the warmth of her skin seeping into my palm—a silent plea for the comfort only I could provide.

"Today is about us," I continued, "and nothing will change that." The promise hung between us, as tangible as the air we breathed. In that moment, I felt my love for her swell within my chest—a fierce tide that would not be quelled by fear or uncertainty.

With a tenderness that belied my form, I wrapped my arms around her slender frame, pulling her close. She fit against me perfectly, as if we were two pieces of a puzzle long separated by cruel fate. Her head rested against my chest, and I could feel her tension begin to melt away under my protective embrace.

As I stroked her hair, each silken strand slipping through my fingers like threads of moonlight, I sensed her worries unraveling. "We are safe," I murmured into the night. "And we will face whatever comes together."

She lifted her face to mine, those brilliant eyes searching for any hint of doubt in my own. But she would find none—I was resolute in my vow to shield her from any harm that dared approach.

I could see it then, the flicker of joy slowly returning to her eyes like the first rays of dawn after a long night. It was all I needed to know that my words had reached her heart.

"We are strong together," I said with quiet conviction. "Stronger than any curse or shadow that lurks beyond these walls."

In our embrace beneath the watchful stars, there was no prince or beast—only two hearts beating as one, ready to stand against whatever trials awaited us with unwavering courage and love.

The grand hall, a testament to the grandeur of our kingdom, blossomed with the hues of a thousand flowers, their petals unfurling like the dawn of our new life together. Sunlight streamed through the stained-glass windows, casting kaleidoscopic patterns upon the faces of our people, who gathered in silent reverence for the union they were about to witness.

I stood before Beauty, my heart a tempest of joy and awe. The walls of the chapel, ancient and steadfast, seemed to lean in, eager to cup the sacredness of this moment within their stone embrace. Her hands, delicate yet strong within my own, were anchors in a sea of emotion that threatened to sweep me away. The amethyst of her gown mirrored the twilight sky that peered through the stained glass, bathing her in a kaleidoscope of light and shadow.

"This is the beginning of our forever," I whispered, the words a sacred oath between us. As I gazed into her eyes, I saw not just the love that had grown between us, blossoming from the seeds of trust and respect, but also the shared trials that had forge our bond in the crucible of fire and ice.

The officiant's voice, soft and resonant, wove around us like a silken ribbon. "Do you, Prince Eirian, take this woman to be your lawfully wedded wife, to have and to hold, in sickness and in health, for richer or for poorer, as long as you both shall live?"

"I do," I said, the words a solemn vow that echoed through the very marrow of my bones. "Together, we will lead and protect our kingdom, with every beat of our hearts and every breath in our lungs. Our paths intertwined, we shall face the dawn of each new day as one. I am yours entirely—no longer a beast ensnared by his own lament, but a man made whole by the transformative power of your love."

Her fingers tightened around mine, a silent affirmation that spoke volumes. With every breath we drew, we wove together the tapestry of our destiny—a tapestry rich with the threads of courage, hope, and an enduring love that had conquered the darkness of my curse.

As she spoke her vows in return, her voice a melody that resonated with the depth of the ages, I knew that every trial we would face henceforth would be met with this same unyielding strength. "Eirian, my love, my dragon prince, I vow to stand by your side through every storm and every sunrise. I will be your partner, your confidant, your greatest ally. Our love will be the beacon that guides our people to brighter futures."

The officiant pronounced us husband and wife, and as our lips met in a kiss that sealed our souls together, a tempest of applause and cheers erupted from those who bore witness to our union. Yet all I could hear was the beating of her heart against mine—a drumbeat of unity and passion that drowned out the world. Two dragons, once alone in their respective skies, now soared side by side, their flames intertwined, painting the heavens with the incandescent glow of their eternal bond.

The grand hall, once a place of somber solitude, now pulsed with life and color, transformed into a festive banquet as if by the wand of a benevolent sorceress. Garlands of flowers hung from the rafters, their petals vibrant against the stone. The air was rich with the scents of roasted meats and sweet pastries, a feast for the senses that rivaled even the most lavish of celebrations in memory.

As Beauty and I entered, hand in hand, a cheer rose from our people. They had gathered here not just as subjects to their rulers, but as witnesses to the enduring power of love and perseverance. Their faces were alight with joy—joy for us, joy for the kingdom, joy for the end of long-held sorrows.

The music swelled, a lively tune that beckoned even the most reticent to the dance floor. And there we were, amidst it all, Beauty and I taking our first dance as husband and wife. "This is what we've fought for," I thought, gazing into her eyes which sparkled brighter than the jewels adorning her gown. Our bodies moved in graceful harmony, a dance that spoke of battles won and hardships overcome.

I held Beauty close, feeling her laughter reverberate against my chest. The unity and joy of our people filled the hall like an enchanting melody. "Our love and leadership will guide us through any challenge," I reflected inwardly, my heart brimming with a sense of invincibility. With her by my side, every dream seemed within reach, every fear surmountable.

As we twirled across the floor, I could hear the clinking of glasses as toasts were made in our honor. We paused to raise our own—a promise to each other and to those we held dear. "To a future bright with hope," I declared, my voice carrying over the crowd.

The guests echoed our sentiment, their voices a harmonious chorus that resonated within the stone walls of our ancestral home. As we continued to dance, I realized that this moment was more than a personal triumph; it was a testament to the enduring spirit of our people.

The laughter and happiness filling the air was not just for us—it was for every heart that dared to dream of peace in times of darkness. It was for every soul that found strength in unity when faced with division.

As Beauty and I danced on into the night, surrounded by friends and family, every step felt like a step into legend—a story that would be told for generations to come. This was not just a celebration; it was an affirmation that together we were stronger than any curse or shadow ever could be.

And as we spun under the tapestry of stars visible through the open windows of the grand hall, I knew with unwavering certainty that no matter what trials lay ahead, our love would endure them all.

In the quiet seclusion of the castle's twilight garden, the din of the day's festivities seemed like a distant dream. Here, in this sanctuary where only the softest whispers of wind and the gentle trickle of a fountain dared to speak, Beauty and I shared a moment of stillness. The lanterns, with their amber glow, bathed us in a warm embrace, lending an ethereal quality to her features.

Her hand lay in mine, a delicate weight that grounded me to this moment, to her. Our fingers intertwined, as naturally as roots seeking soil, finding nourishment in each other's presence. I lifted her hand to my lips, feeling the thrum of her pulse against my kiss—a rhythm that matched the beating of my own heart.

"We are unstoppable together," I found myself murmuring, my voice a soft echo in the vastness of our joined souls. The trials we had faced—beasts of flame and treacherous ice—were testament to the strength that lay in our union. Yet here, beneath the crescent moon's watchful eye, it was not our might that filled me with awe; it was the quiet certainty of our bond.

Beauty's gaze met mine, a mirror reflecting back all that I felt but could not put into words. The depth there was immeasurable; it spoke of battles yet to come and whispered promises yet to be fulfilled. With a gentleness that belied the power she wielded as a dragon shifter, she brushed a strand of hair from my brow.

"For our kingdom, for our future," I whispered against her forehead before pressing my lips there in a tender kiss. It was a seal upon our commitment—a vow that transcended any spoken oath. In her eyes, I saw not just my queen but my partner in every sense—the one with whom I would forge a path through whatever darkness might loom on our horizon.

As we stood there, hand in hand, I knew we were ready. Ready to face any challenge, to uphold the destiny that was ours by right and by choice. Our love was more than a mere feeling; it was a force—a source of strength and resilience that would guide us through storms and stillness alike.

In the tranquility of that garden, with Beauty by my side, contentment enveloped me like a cloak woven from peace itself. We had weathered much together, she and I. The fires of adversity had tempered us; we had emerged not hardened but made whole by each other's presence.

And as we turned back toward the castle—the stronghold of our future reign—I felt an unshakeable resolve settle within me. Together we would lead; together we would protect this kingdom we called home. With Beauty beside me, there was nothing we could not face.

The night deepened around us as we made our way back through the garden's fragrant embrace. In this hushed hour before dawn's first light, I knew one thing with unwavering certainty: united in love and purpose, Beauty and I were indeed unstoppable.

New Dawn, New Hope

Beauty

A few months after our wedding, I awoke with the first rays of dawn filtering through the sheer curtains, casting a soft, golden glow across the royal chambers. The room was quiet, save for the distant song of a lark greeting the new day. As I stretched beneath the silken sheets, I felt an unfamiliar sensation—a subtle queasiness that stirred in my stomach, accompanied by a weariness that seemed to weigh upon my limbs.

"Something feels different today," I murmured to myself, my thoughts still hazy from sleep. The unfamiliar feelings prompted a mix of curiosity and a flicker of joy within me. With each slow breath, I tried to understand this change that whispered through my body.

Lying there in the comforting embrace of my bed, I allowed my hand to drift to my abdomen, a sense of wonder blooming alongside the mild discomfort. "Maybe it's just stress," I pondered aloud, though the corners of my lips turned upward at the thought that it could be something more—a new beginning taking root.

The notion filled me with a warmth that rivaled the sun's gentle caress. My heart fluttered with hope and excitement as I considered the possibility that life within me might have sparked into being. It was a prospect both thrilling and daunting.

Yet amidst this budding joy, there was also a whisper of anxiety—a trepidation about what such a change would mean for Eirian and me. We had faced so much together, our love forging a path through curses and battles. Could we now be standing on the cusp of yet another profound journey?

I sat up slowly, pushing aside the covers as I took stock of myself. The queasiness persisted, but so did the undercurrent of elation. Rising from the bed, I resolved to seek out the castle's healer. There were questions in my heart that needed answers—questions that might very well shape our future.

With each step toward the healer's quarters, my anticipation grew. What news would she have for me? Would she confirm what my heart dared to hope? The stone corridors seemed to echo with the beat of my racing pulse as I made my way through the castle, driven by a need to know if indeed a new life was blossoming within me—a life that would bind Eirian and me even closer together and herald a new chapter in our shared story.

The sun climbed higher in the sky, casting its rays into every corner of the castle as I made my way to the healer's quarters. My footsteps echoed through the halls, a rhythmic beat that seemed to keep time with the thrumming of my heart. With each step, my mind spun with possibilities, a kaleidoscope of hope and trepidation that colored my thoughts.

The healer's room was a sanctuary of knowledge and comfort, the walls lined with shelves brimming with jars of herbs and vials of potions. The scent of lavender and chamomile hung in the air, a soothing balm to my frayed nerves. I watched as she laid out her tools with practiced ease, her hands steady and sure.

"Good morning, my lady," she greeted me with a warm smile that did little to quell the fluttering in my stomach. "What brings you here today?"

I took a deep breath, gathering my courage before speaking. "I've been feeling... different," I began, hesitating as I searched for the right words. "There's a queasiness that lingers and a fatigue that weighs upon me."

The healer nodded thoughtfully, her eyes taking on a spark of understanding as she motioned for me to sit. "Let us see what we can discern," she said softly, her voice carrying the wisdom of years spent tending to others.

As I sat on the edge of the table, I felt exposed under her knowing gaze. She moved with gentle precision, her fingers probing gently as she murmured words too low for me to catch. The room was quiet save for the rustle of her robes and the gentle motion of her hands.

"What could this mean?" I wondered silently, trying to still the anxious thoughts that clamored for attention. My eyes followed her every move, searching for any hint of what she might find.

The healer paused in her examination, meeting my gaze with an enigmatic smile that set my heart racing anew. "Please," I whispered under my breath, a silent plea for good news.

She reached for a small vial filled with a clear liquid and uncorked it carefully before offering it to me. "Drink this," she instructed. "It will help settle your stomach while we wait."

I complied without question, the cool potion sliding down my throat and spreading a sense of calm through my body. As we waited for the effects to take hold, an air of anticipation settled around us like a cloak.

"Whatever comes next," I thought as I braced myself for her verdict, "I am ready." My hands rested protectively over my stomach, instinctively cradling the potential life within as I awaited the healer's words with bated breath.

The healer's room, nestled within the royal chambers, had always been a place of solace and healing. But today, as I sat upon the plush stool, draped in a soft shawl against the morning chill, it felt like the stage for a momentous revelation.

"Congratulations, my lady, you are with child." The healer's voice was gentle, her eyes warm with shared joy.

A gasp escaped my lips before I could catch it. My hand, trembling with a life of its own, found its way to my abdomen. Beneath my palm, I imagined the tiny spark of new life that had taken root within me. "A baby... we're going to have a baby," I whispered, my voice a mixture of wonder and disbelief.

Tears blurred my vision as I looked up at the healer. She offered me a tender smile, reaching out to squeeze my hand in reassurance. The room spun around me in a whirlwind of emotion—shock at the unexpected news, joy at the thought of the life Eirian and I would bring into this world, and an undercurrent of anxiety about the unknowns that lay ahead.

"This changes everything," I realized as the weight of motherhood settled upon my shoulders—a mantle I was both honored and daunted to wear. The love for this unborn child swelled within me like a tide, filling every crevice of my heart with light and warmth.

The healer's voice brought me back to the present. "You must take care now, more than ever," she advised with an air of solemnity. "The life you carry is precious and will need your strength."

I nodded, absorbing her words. My thoughts drifted to Eirian—my beloved, who had stood by me through trials by fire and ice. How would he react to our miracle? Anticipation quickened my pulse as I envisioned sharing this joyous news with him.

As I rose from the stool, steadied by the healer's hand on my elbow, I felt a profound sense of connection—to the life burgeoning within me, to Eirian, whose love had become my anchor, and to our kingdom that we would soon see flourish anew.

With each step back towards our chambers where Eirian awaited me, my heart sang with newfound purpose. Today marked not just another dawn but the beginning of an extraordinary journey that Eirian and I would embark on together—as partners, as rulers, and now as parents.

The door to our chambers loomed before me—a threshold that would lead me into Eirian's embrace and into the future we would build for our child. Taking a deep breath to steady myself against the swell of emotions within me, I pushed open the door and stepped into the light.

The castle gardens were a sanctuary of tranquility, where the riotous colors of blooming flowers mingled with the serene whispers of rustling leaves. I found Eirian there, standing amidst the verdant greenery, his gaze lost in the contemplation of a delicate rose. His silhouette, framed by the soft morning light, was a testament to the peace we had fought so hard to achieve.

My heart pounded with a rhythm that matched the fluttering wings of the butterflies dancing around us. "Eirian," I called out softly, my voice barely rising above the gentle hum of the garden.

He turned at the sound of my voice, his expression shifting from quiet reflection to bright attentiveness. "Beauty," he greeted me, his eyes lighting up with warmth and love.

I approached him, my steps hesitant as I closed the distance between us. The news I carried felt like a fragile bird nestled in my chest—eager to take flight yet vulnerable in its significance.

"I have something to tell you," I began, my voice trembling with the weight of emotion that filled me. The words hung in the air between us, charged with anticipation.

Eirian's gaze searched mine, a hint of concern etching his noble features. "What is it, my love?" he asked, reaching out to take my hands in his.

Taking a deep breath, I let the truth spill forth like a stream breaking free from winter's hold. "I am with child," I whispered, watching as understanding dawned in his eyes.

For a moment, time seemed to stand still as Eirian processed my words. Then, as if released from a spell, his face broke into an expression of pure joy. His eyes widened with delight and wonder—the kind that mirrored the awe-inspiring magic we had witnessed together on our journey.

"We're going to have a baby," he murmured, his voice brimming with wonder and tenderness. With a swift movement born of elation, he lifted me into his arms and spun me around in a dizzying embrace.

Laughter bubbled up from within me—a cascade of happiness that overflowed and mingled with Eirian's own joyous chuckles. As he set me down gently upon the soft grass, our eyes met and held—a silent conversation that spoke volumes of our shared love and devotion.

"We're going to be parents," I thought to myself as reality settled around us like dew upon morning petals. This precious moment marked not just the beginning of new life but also a deepening of our bond—one that had been forged in fire and tempered by trials.

Eirian's arms enveloped me once more, drawing me close against his chest where I could hear the steady beat of his heart—a rhythm that now held new promise for both our futures. In this serene garden where life bloomed unabated, we stood together at the threshold of an extraordinary new chapter—one filled with hope and dreams yet to unfold.

The grand hall of the castle was aglow with a hundred flickering candles, casting a golden sheen over the faces of the assembled crowd. The air hummed with anticipation, and I could feel the collective heartbeat of our kingdom reverberating through the stone floor beneath my feet. Eirian stood beside me, his hand a reassuring weight on the small of my back as we prepared to share our news.

"We have joyous news to share," I began, my voice echoing off the vaulted ceilings. A hush fell over the crowd, every eye trained on us. I drew in a steadying breath, feeling Eirian's presence like a pillar of strength at my side. "We are expecting a child."

The response was immediate—a cacophony of cheers and applause that swelled like a wave crashing against the shore. The joy was palpable, filling the hall with an energy that seemed to sparkle in the air itself. I met Eirian's eyes, finding within them a reflection of all the love and support that now wrapped around us like a warm embrace.

As the clamor subsided into excited murmurs and shared congratulations, I felt a smile spread across my face, genuine and bright. "This child will be our future," I thought, filled with hope and pride.

Eirian squeezed my hand, and I turned to look at him once more, his face alight with happiness.

Together we faced our people, united not just by love but by purpose. We were their leaders, their protectors, and now we would be parents to the heir who would one day carry on our legacy. It was a responsibility that weighed heavily but one that we bore gladly—for this child symbolized more than just an addition to our family; they were a beacon of hope for a kingdom that had seen too much darkness.

As we descended from the dais to mingle with our subjects, their well-wishes enveloped us like the softest cloak. There were handshakes and hugs, laughter and tears—all expressions of a shared joy that transcended rank or station.

I moved through the crowd, Eirian always within reach, and each face I saw bore a smile—a testament to the love they had for their prince and their newfound affection for me. It was in this moment that I truly understood what it meant to be part of something greater than myself—to be woven into the fabric of this kingdom's history and its future.

The royal chambers were a sanctuary, bathed in the soft glow of twilight that seeped through the arched windows. As Eirian and I prepared for bed, the quiet rustle of silk and the gentle clinking of armor being set aside were the only sounds that dared disturb the hush of evening. The world outside our walls was fraught with shadows and whispers of danger, but within these walls, we found solace in each other's presence.

I watched Eirian as he moved with a grace that belied his strength, his hands carefully placing his sword upon its stand—a silent sentinel in the corner of our room. There was a peace to his actions, a ritual that grounded him after a day filled with the weight of a crown. As he turned to face me, our eyes met, and in his gaze, I found an ocean of unspoken words.

He approached me then, taking my hands in his. The warmth of his touch seeped into my skin, a stark contrast to the coolness of the evening air that whispered through the open window. "Whatever comes," he said, his voice a low rumble that resonated within the chamber and within my heart, "we will face it together."

His words wrapped around me like a cloak, fortifying my spirit. I nodded, feeling the truth of his promise reverberate through every fiber of my being. "Together, we are unstoppable," I replied, leaning into him and finding comfort in the solid reality of his embrace.

His arms encircled me, strong and sure—a bastion against any storm that might rage against us. And there we stood, two halves of a whole, united by love and bound by a shared destiny. Our hearts beat in tandem—a rhythm that pulsed with love and determination to protect not just each other but also the kingdom we held dear.

"For our family, for our kingdom," I thought as I closed my eyes and rested my head against Eirian's chest. His heartbeat was a lullaby that soothed away any lingering fears and filled me with an overwhelming sense of peace.

The chamber's soft lighting cast gentle shadows upon the walls—shadows that danced with the flicker of candlelight but held no menace. They were but phantoms of light and dark, playing out their silent performance as witnesses to our promise.

And as we embraced in the quietude of our chambers—two souls entwined by love and shared purpose—I knew that no matter what challenges lay ahead, we would face them together. For in each other's arms, we found not only refuge but also an unyielding strength that would carry us through whatever tomorrow might bring.

The castle was draped in silence, a stark contrast to the revelry of the day. As I stood by the window of our chambers, gazing out at the moonlit landscape, an eerie stillness hung heavy in the air. Eirian's steady breathing behind me was a comforting lullaby against the night's quietude. But something tugged at the edges of my consciousness—a whisper of unease that refused to be ignored.

A chill skittered down my spine, raising goosebumps on my arms. It was as if the night itself had suddenly drawn a cold breath, and with it came the sense of an ominous presence lurking just beyond sight. I wrapped my arms around myself, a futile attempt to ward off the sudden drop in temperature and the growing trepidation.

"She's still out there," I thought, my gaze scanning the shadows that clung to the castle walls and crept among the forest's edge. The darkness seemed alive, watching, waiting—a predator poised in anticipation. My resolve hardened like ice within my veins; this shadowy threat had been a silent specter, a constant reminder that peace was often fragile.

I placed a protective hand on my abdomen, feeling the faint flutter that connected me to the new life growing inside me—a life that Eirian and I had created out of love and hope in a world that seemed determined to test our strength at every turn. "I will keep you safe," I whispered into the stillness, my voice carrying the weight of a vow.

The protective instincts that had carried me through battles and heartache surged anew, filling me with a strength that was both fierce and tender. With every fiber of my being, I would guard this child, our future—just as Eirian and I would stand together against any darkness that dared to threaten our kingdom.

I drew back from the window, unwilling to let fear take root in my heart. Instead, I chose to focus on the warmth of our bedchamber, where Eirian slept peacefully, unaware of my midnight vigil. The sight of him—so strong yet so vulnerable in repose—steeled my resolve even further.

Turning away from the night's chill embrace, I slipped back into bed beside him. As I nestled close against his side, drawing comfort from his presence, I knew that whatever challenges lay ahead, we would face them together—with courage, with love, and with an unyielding determination to protect our family and our people.

Legacy Renewed

Prince Eirian

I awoke with a start, a cold dread creeping over me. The castle was shrouded in darkness, each shadow seeming to pulse with menace. *Something's not right,* I thought, slipping out of bed quietly so as not to disturb Beauty. Her peaceful breathing was the only sound in the otherwise silent chamber, a stark contrast to the turmoil brewing within me.

As I moved through the dark hallways, my senses were heightened, every shadow an abyss from which danger might spring. *I have to find the source,* I resolved, feeling the weight of my responsibility pressing down on me like the stone blocks of the castle walls. The love for Beauty and our unborn child fueled my determination to protect them.

The air was chill, a whisper of frost that seemed unnatural even for this late hour. It brushed against my skin, raising goosebumps—a herald of something sinister infiltrating our sanctuary. With each step, my dragon instincts roared to life, ready to defend, to burn away the shadows with fire should it be necessary.

I reached the grand staircase, its ornate railings lost in gloom. A draft stirred from below, carrying with it a scent that set my nerves on edge—a trace of dark magic, faint but unmistakable. It was a smell I knew all too well from battles past; it was the stench of Freya's sorcery.

I descended with caution, prepared to summon flame. My heart thundered in my chest—not with fear, but with fierce resolve. Whatever lurked in the depths of my home would find that Prince Eirian was no easy prey.

At the bottom of the stairs, I paused. The great hall lay ahead, its vast doors slightly ajar. Beyond them lay darkness so profound it seemed alive, hungry. *She's here,* I realized with grim certainty.

With a silent prayer for strength and protection over Beauty and our child, I pushed open the doors and stepped into the abyss beyond. The darkness wrapped around me like a shroud; even my enhanced vision could barely pierce it.

Show yourself, I commanded silently to whatever hid within the shadows. *I am ready for you.*

The castle's ancient archives always held a sense of foreboding, as if the knowledge within was guarded by the spirits of the past. But tonight, the air was thicker, charged with a sinister energy that seemed to hum through the stone walls. *Freya's handiwork,* I mused darkly as I ran my fingers over the spines of dusty tomes, searching for anything that could shed light on the shadow that had invaded our home.

My heart was a drumbeat in my chest, pounding out a rhythm of fear and determination. With every step deeper into the labyrinth of shelves and scrolls, the shadow's presence grew more oppressive, as if it were a living thing, feeding on my unease.

Then I saw it—an ancient manuscript bound in leather so dark it seemed to swallow the weak candlelight. The book's clasp was an emblem I knew all too well: a serpent coiled around a scepter, Freya's mark. A shiver ran down my spine as I reached out and touched it, feeling an immediate rush of coldness that seeped into my bones.

I carefully opened the manuscript to pages filled with spidery script and diagrams of arcane symbols. My eyes scanned the text, deciphering words that spoke of curses and shadows, of magic twisted into forms meant to torment and control. And there it was—a passage describing a wraith born from darkness, an extension of the caster's will sent to hunt and harry their prey.

"This shadow... it's connected to her curse," I whispered into the silence, realization dawning like ice forming on glass. The air around me seemed to respond, growing colder still, as if Freya herself were watching me uncover her secrets.

It wasn't over yet; this shadow was but a harbinger of what was to come. My thoughts raced—how could I protect Beauty and our child from a threat woven from darkness itself? *We've come too far to let this destroy us.* I felt the dragon within me stir, its fiery heart defiant against the creeping chill.

As the candlelight flickered, casting a weak glow over the manuscript's aged pages, I felt the shadows in the ancient archives press closer, as if eager to read over my shoulder. My fingers traced the elegant script that detailed the remnants of Freya's dark sorcery. The weight of the castle above me seemed to grow heavier with each word, a physical manifestation of the threat that loomed over us all.

"This shadow could jeopardize everything we've built," I murmured to myself, the words tasting like ash on my tongue. My thoughts immediately flew to Beauty, her smile that could banish any darkness, and our unborn child—a beacon of hope for our future. The idea of any harm coming to them ignited a surge of protectiveness within me that burned hotter than any dragon fire.

We had thought ourselves victorious, that love and unity had conquered Freya's icy grip. Yet here I was, faced with evidence that her curse lingered like a parasite, feeding off the remnants of her malice. It was clear we had celebrated too soon; the battle was not over.

"We need to prepare," I whispered into the oppressive silence of the archives. My dragon's heart thrummed within my chest, ready to rise up and defend what was mine—what was ours. With each heartbeat, my resolve hardened like steel forged in dragon flame.

I carefully turned another page, seeking knowledge that would help us counter this new threat. My mind raced with strategies, plans unfurling like wings at dawn. "We'll find a way to dispel this darkness," I vowed silently.

The shadows seemed to recoil as if they could hear my thoughts and feared them. Good. Let them fear, for they would soon learn that

Prince Eirian and his queen were more than mere tales sung by bards; we were a force that would not yield to darkness or despair.

With one last look at the manuscript—a guide now etched into my memory—I stood up. The candlelight flickered one final time before being snuffed out by an errant draft, plunging me into darkness.

But I was not afraid. The shadows could not touch me—not when my heart carried its own brilliant light. Clutching the manuscript close, I made my way back through the labyrinthine corridors of my ancestral home, each step a silent promise to Beauty and our child: no shadow would cast its pall over our kingdom again. Not while I drew breath and fire burned in my veins.

I crept into the royal chambers, where moonlight streamed through the windows, casting a serene glow over Beauty's sleeping form. My heart swelled with love and an ache that ran deeper than the marrow of my bones. I knew I had to wake her, yet part of me longed to let her rest, to shield her from the shadows that threatened our hard-won peace.

"We need to talk," I whispered, my voice barely a breath as I gently shook her shoulder. Her eyes fluttered open, and in them, I saw the stars of our shared destiny. The sight of her gave me courage, even as my chest tightened with the weight of what I had to say.

"Love," I began, the term of endearment slipping naturally from my lips, "there's a shadow in our midst—a remnant of Freya's curse." Her gaze didn't waver; it was as if she had always known our trials were far from over.

I told her everything—the chill of dark magic in the air, the manuscript that held secrets bound in malice, and how this new threat loomed over our family like a storm cloud. As I spoke, Beauty sat up, wrapping her arms around herself against the chill that seemed to emanate from my tale.

"We'll face this together," I assured her. Her hand found mine, and in that simple touch was a fortress of strength. "We can't let it harm our family or kingdom." The words were as much a vow to myself as they were a promise to her.

Her fingers tightened around mine. "I know we will," she said, her voice firm with conviction. It was that same unwavering spirit that had first bridged the distance between us—that had transformed me not just in flesh but in soul.

I drew from her strength as much as she did from mine. Together we had faced trials that would have shattered lesser bonds. And now, as we prepared for this new challenge, I felt our unity solidify into something unbreakable.

"She's my strength," I thought as we rose together from the bed. "And together we're unstoppable." The shadows could gather and darkness could whisper its lies, but they would never find purchase in the light of our resolve.

In the quiet sanctum of our royal chambers, the world outside faded to a mere whisper against the thick stone walls. Beauty and I stood hand in hand, the soft glow of the bedside candles casting dancing shadows upon the walls. The light played upon her features, accentuating the determination set upon her brow and the love that lived in her eyes—mirrors of my own heart.

"No matter what comes, we will face it together," I said, my voice a low rumble, as steady and sure as the earth beneath our feet. Our intertwined fingers were a tangible testament to the strength we drew from one another.

She nodded, her grip tightening. "I know we will," she replied, her voice a soothing balm to the storm of worries brewing within me. "Together, we are stronger than any curse, any shadow that dares to threaten our peace."

As we prepared for bed that night, I couldn't help but let my thoughts drift toward our future—the child who would soon join us in this world. Would they inherit the dragon's might or the steadfast courage of their mother? Would they grow up under the shadow of Freya's malice or in a kingdom renewed by hope?

These questions circled in my mind like moths to flame, yet as I looked into Beauty's eyes, I found my fears quelled. "Together, we are unstoppable," I whispered more to myself than to her. A sense of peace enveloped me, cocooning us in its gentle embrace.

We embraced then, our bodies fitting together as if two halves of a whole. Her warmth seeped into my very bones, and for a moment, all was right with the world. "For our child, for our kingdom, we will fight," I vowed silently against her hair.

And as we lay down to rest beneath silken sheets and whispered promises into the night, I knew that whatever darkness lay ahead would find us unyielding. For in each other, we had found an ally stronger than any foe—a love that transcended curses and fate itself.

In this room where secrets and plans had been shared and futures dreamt up, Beauty and I reaffirmed our commitment not just to each other but to the very essence of what made us who we were. With profound love and unwavering determination etched into every word spoken and every silent pledge made in the stillness of our chambers, we drifted into sleep with hearts full and spirits undaunted.

The air within our chamber was thick with the warmth of hearth and the scent of a thousand delicate flowers—a sanctuary crafted by Beauty's own will, a place that had come to embody the depth of our love. It was here, amidst the echoes of our shared laughter and whispered dreams, that we would welcome a new life into the world.

The first tremors of labor gripped Beauty in the quiet of night, when the stars outside our window were the only audience to her courage. I was at her side in an instant, my hand enveloping hers—a silent vow that I would be her anchor through the tempests to come.

"Eirian," she gasped, her fingers like delicate claws against my palm, "it's time."

"I am here, my love," I murmured, my voice a steady drumbeat amidst the chaos of our preparations. Midwives flitted about the room, their movements a dance of precision and urgency, but all I saw was Beauty—her strength, her resolve, her beauty transcending the pain that etched itself upon her features.

The hours slipped by, marked by the rhythmic dance of candlelight and the shallow rise and fall of Beauty's chest. Sweat beaded upon her brow, and I brushed it away with the tender reverence one might reserve for the most sacred of rites.

"You're so strong," I whispered against the shell of her ear, my heart a symphony of awe and love. Her response was a grimace that bore the weight of our future, a future that now quickened within her.

I cannot say how many times the moon arced its path across the night sky, nor can I recount the moments of doubt that clawed at the edges of my mind. But as the first light of dawn crept beneath the curtains, a new sound filled the room—a cry, small and insistent, that heralded the arrival of our son.

In that moment, the world stilled. The air, once heavy with the effort of birth, seemed to shimmer with the clarity of new beginnings. I lifted our child into my arms and was struck by the sheer wonder of creation.

"We did it," I thought, my voice breaking with emotion as I gazed upon his tiny, perfect face. His cries were music to my ears, a testament to the resilience of life—of our love.

"He's perfect," I whispered, my eyes meeting Beauty's over the bundle in my arms. Her smile, weary yet radiant, was all the confirmation I needed. This child was the embodiment of our journey, a living symbol of hope and unity.

"This is our future," I vowed silently, the words engraving themselves upon my soul. As I placed our son against Beauty's chest, I felt the last of my doubts melt away. The shadows that had once threatened to consume me were now but distant memories, powerless against the light of our family's love.

In the hushed aftermath of our son's arrival, the world seemed to hold its breath. The royal chambers, once a place of solitude and reflection, had transformed into a cradle of new life and whispered promises. I stood there, cradling the tiny, miraculous being who had so recently entered our world, his breaths small puffs of wonder against my skin.

"We will protect you," I whispered, the words a sacred oath that bound me more firmly than any spell. My gaze lifted to meet Beauty's, her eyes luminous with love and a touch of exhaustion. In her gaze, I found an echo of my own resolve, a shared understanding that our lives had irrevocably changed.

"For our family, for our kingdom," I thought, the weight of the crown upon my brow a distant memory compared to the weight of the child in my arms. The shadow of the prophecy, once a dark cloud upon our horizon, now mingled with the soft glow of hope that suffused the room.

I felt a surge of determination, a renewed sense of purpose that steeled my resolve. "We will face whatever comes," I vowed silently, the promise as much for myself as for the tiny life we had brought into this world. The prophecy's whispers, though muted by the joy of the moment, remained a constant reminder that our journey was far from over.

Beauty reached out, her fingers brushing against the downy softness of our son's cheek, and I saw in her touch a future filled with promise. "He's so small," she said, her voice a tender melody in the quiet of the room.

"Yet he holds the strength of both our lineages," I replied, my words a quiet acknowledgment of the power that now lay in our arms—a power that we would nurture and guide as he grew.

We spoke then of our hopes and dreams, our voices intertwining in the stillness as we wove a tapestry of possibilities for our son's life. We imagined the world he would one day inherit, a kingdom no longer bound by the chains of winter or the specter of ancient feuds.

The prophecy might speak of trials to come, but in that moment, it was the love we held for our child that filled the room, a love so vast and all-encompassing that it seemed to quiet the very winds that had once howled against our doors.

I knew that the road ahead would be fraught with challenges, that the peace we now enjoyed was but a brief respite in a world that would soon demand much of us. But as I stood there, with Beauty by my side and our son cradled in my arms, I felt a sense of rightness, a deep-seated conviction that together, we could meet any adversity.

The soft lighting cast a warm glow over the scene, gilding the edges of our new existence. I looked down at the child who had so changed my world, and I saw in his face the promise of a new dawn.

"We will teach you the ways of our people," I murmured, my voice carrying the weight of my promise. "We will show you how to soar above the trials of life, to find strength in adversity, and to lead with both wisdom and compassion."

As our eyes met once more over the cherished bundle of our son, Beauty and I shared a look that spoke volumes—a look that needed no words, for our hearts beat in unison, bound by the sacred vows we had spoken and the love that would guide us into the future.

The chapter of our lives that had begun with a curse was now unfolding into a tale of redemption and hope. With our son as the bridge between our past and our future, we were ready to face whatever trials lay ahead, our bond unbreakable, our determination unwavering.

And so, with hearts full and spirits eager, we stepped forward into the light of our new beginning, a family forged by love and destined to shape the world.

In this moment of peace and promise, the narrative of our lives took a turn toward a future replete with potential and possibility. Here, in the quiet sanctuary of our royal chambers, we found the strength to face the unknown, our resolve bolstered by the precious life we had created—a symbol of our enduring love and the unity that would guide our kingdom to a bright and hopeful era.

Read the first book in my Enchanted Ever Afters fairy tale romance series *The Sword and the Slipper*

A forbidden love, a dangerous secret, and a kingdom teetering on the edge of ruin. As a celebrated dragon slayer, I've faced countless dangers to protect my kingdom. Disguised as a noble, I infiltrate a royal ball to uncover the sinister forces behind recent dragon attacks. What I didn't expect was to find my heart ensnared by a mysterious beauty. Dreaming of freedom and love, she attends the royal ball with the help of a magical transformation, and our worlds collide in a dance of passion and intrigue. As sparks fly between us, we must navigate dangerous secrets that threaten to tear us apart. With the kingdom's future hanging in the balance, our love becomes the key to unraveling a deadly conspiracy. In a land where love and magic intertwine, only our bond can save the kingdom from the shadows of the past.

What people are saying:

Another amazing page turner 5 stars

This is a retelling of the Cinderella classic with a twist. Full of danger, dragons, and suspense. An amazing story with wonderful characters and an intriguing storyline that's truly enjoyable. Highly recommend reading this book. Luna Rains has delivered another amazing page turner and I look forward to reading more.

Cinderella with a dragon twist 5 stars

This is a Cinderella retelling with a dragon twist. Great book! It pulled me in from beginning to end and held my attention. The world building is detailed and imaginative. This book has strong, well-developed characters, an interesting story line full of suspense, danger, action, mystery, unexpected twists, and an ending that left me wanting to read more.

The Sword & the Slipper 5 stars

A beautiful retelling of Cinderella that I found more intriguing than the original!

Magical re-telling 5 stars

This retelling of the classic Cinderella is jam-packed with twists, turns and secrets. This is must read book!

Dragon Shifter Cinderella Tale 4 stars

The classic tale of Cinderella, with a bit of a twist. There are dragons attacking the kingdom, but who's behind it and why? Are Cinderella's stepmother and sister truly dragons?

Don't miss out!

Visit the website below and you can sign up to receive emails whenever Luna Rains publishes a new book. There's no charge and no obligation.

https://books2read.com/r/B-A-VUJHB-NNHTE

Connecting independent readers to independent writers.

Also by Luna Rains

Enchanted Ever Afters
The Arrow and the Axe

Fated Mates Saga
Fated Mate Surprise Daddy
Fated Mate Triplets Daddy
Fated Mate Secret Babies
Fated Mate Secret Twin
Fated Mate Twins Reunited
Fated Mate Witch's Prophecy
Fated Mate Prophecy Fulfilled

Shifter Royals: Fairy Tale Fated Mates
The Dragon's Magical Mate
Beauty and the Dragon Beast

Standalone
The Sword & the slipper

Watch for more at https://jllampublishing.com.

About the Author

I am Luna Rains, a romance author raised amid the enchanting allure of the southern landscape. My roots are deeply entwined in the mysteries of the South, and my novels exude an irresistible blend of paranormal fascination and scorching passion.

Hailing from a small Georgia town, my upbringing amidst ancient oaks and whispered legends fueled my imagination. Savannah, my hometown, is known as the most haunted city in the country. Now in my thriving thirties, I channel my intrigue for the unknown into spellbinding tales of ethereal love. My novels entwine spectral beings with unbridled desire, painting a world where love defies both time and the supernatural.

With a devoted following, I have mastered the art of kindling flames through my paranormal romance stories, etching my name as a maestro of the genre. My passion for crafting tales that blend the mystical with the sensual has become my signature, and I take pride in transporting my readers to realms where love knows no bounds.

Read more at https://jllampublishing.com.